SLAUGHTER IN SINGAPORE

Slaughter in Singapore

Duncan Harding

severn
House

This first world edition published in Great Britain 2003 by
SEVERN HOUSE PUBLISHERS LTD of
9–15 High Street, Sutton, Surrey SM1 1DF.
This first world edition published in the USA 2003 by
SEVERN HOUSE PUBLISHERS INC of
595 Madison Avenue, New York, N.Y. 10022.

British Library Cataloguing in Publication Data

Harding, Duncan, 1926-
    Slaughter in Singapore. - (X-craft)
    1.   World War, 1939-1945 - Naval operations, British - Fiction
    2.   War stories
    I.   Title
    823.9'14 [F]

    ISBN 0-7278-5885-8

Typeset by Palimpsest Book Production Ltd.,
Polmont, Stirlingshire, Scotland.
Printed and bound in Great Britain by
MPG Books Ltd., Bodmin, Cornwall.

'Dictators ride to and fro on tigers which they dare not dismount . . . and the tigers are getting hungry.'

Winston Churchill

X-Craft

I

The Sleeping Beauty

The first operational 'Sleeping Beauty' was delivered to the Royal Marine Boom Detachment (a cover name) at Southsea, England in June 1943. It was a type of electrically powered canoe intended for raiding enemy coasts. It had a range of 20km submerged, but at 4.5 knots on the surface it could cover three times that distance. It could, in addition, ride out a Force Four wind and drive through waves two to three metres high. In short the Sleeping Beauty was an ideal craft for raiding German and Japanese-held coasts.

It is known that the Sleeping Beauty was employed in Operation Malay Tiger against the Japanese in Singapore Harbour. Thereafter secrecy reigned about its further use. However, it is believed that the 'Special Boat Service', the seaborne arm of the British SAS, employs a further development of the Sleeping Beauty to this day. *DH.*

Prelude

The bandy-legged Japanese officer, trailing his absurdly long sword behind him in the dust, swaggered to the front of the prisoners. They knelt, with a rope tied around their wrists and twisted over their necks and pulled very tight so that their heads were bowed in that position of submission which the little men standing waiting under the rising sun flag loved.

The observer couldn't see their faces clearly, but he could smell their abject fear and he could guess, yellow, white and brown, the features of the men about to die so cruelly would be haggard and terrified. He knew his would. He chewed harder on the betel nut and then spat a stream of brown juice to the dust in the coolie fashion. The hot baking earth swallowed the liquid in an instant; it was that hot. Even the light breeze which swept across Singapore's harbour did little to relieve that terrible, oppressive, heat.

'Speedo . . . speedo . . .! You bloody move . . . *speedo!*' the Japanese officer yelled at the last of the prisoners, two slouch-hatted Australians, being prodded to join the rest of those to be executed. Their khaki uniforms were ragged and black with sweat and their eyes were wild with fear, yet they would not bend their heads in submission like the others waiting for the inevitable.

'Good on you, cobbers,' the observer muttered under

his breath and then when he saw one of the Jap guards looking his way, he bowed rapidly, so low that his yellow skin showed through the tears in his ancient khaki shorts, the only garment he wore.

Breathing hard, the two Australian privates were thrust into the centre of the group, not more than ten yards away from the strutting little officer in his brilliant white open-necked shirt and gleaming top boots. The guards attempted to make the Australians bow to the officer, prodding them with their bayonets. But the Aussies, condemned to death as they were, weren't having it. 'Frig that for a game o' soldiers!'

The bigger of the two snarled and yelped with sudden pain the next moment as the guard thrust his bayonet between his ribs. He staggered and would have fallen if his mate hadn't held him, crying, 'Stand fast, Bluey. The fuckers'll pay for this one.'

Grimly the observer, propped up on the side of his ancient Raleigh bike, his pride and joy and sole possession in this world, nodded. 'You betcha, cobber,' he whispered under his breath. Next instant he caught his breath. The Jap officer was pulling out his samurai sword, making a great play of it and, in the sudden absolute silence, the observer could hear the keen blade slither the length of the ancient sheath.

The officer smiled maliciously at the two Australians, who had been forced down on their knees too now. Slowly, very slowly, he wet the thumb of his left hand. Carefully, he started to slide the thumb the length of the obviously razor-sharp sword, dark eyes sparkling behind his tortoiseshell glasses, as if he were enjoying the sensation; almost as if it had some kind of obscene sexual charge.

The observer swallowed hard. He knew what was

coming. In the year since the Japanese had occupied the one-time great Imperial bastion of Singapore, they had terrorized the population, white, brown and yellow, with their atrocities. Not a week had gone by without the Nips slaughtering some poor unfortunate. Today's executions were for a purpose and not the usual murder for the sake of murder. The Japs were taking their revenge for the craft that had been sunk in the great harbour only the week before. Everywhere under the sign of that hated 'fried egg' – their national rising sun flag – they had announced in half a dozen languages that they would show no mercy to those found committing what they thought was sabotage. For how else could those freighters and the little naval vessel have been sunk? As they boasted time and time again over Singapore Radio. *'We are all comrades and co-workers in the Asian Co-Productive Alliance. The cruel English Imperialists will never return. So work together, dear comrades and co-workers for the future of Asia. Eradicate all traitors, English agents and saboteurs. Show no mercy to the running dogs of the English!'*

The officer was obviously satisfied that his sword was sharp enough for the murderous task ahead of him. In a deep guttural voice that sounded something like the hoarse barking of an angry dog, he shouted something at the men guarding the two Australian soldiers. They were slow to respond, it seemed. The fat corporal, his round pig-like face gleaming with sweat, as if it had been greased with vaseline, turned on them. He slapped first the one and then the other hard – so hard that their heads swung to one side and a sudden red finger mark appeared on their dark faces.

Now they grabbed the Australians by their collars. Cruelly they forced their heads forward, baring their skinny necks, the result of months of starvation rations as Japanese prisoners.

The officer grinned with pleasure. His teeth gleamed like in a pre-war ad for Colgate toothpaste. He raised his sword high above his shaven head. The observer could see the twin patches of black sweat under his armpits. He brought it down slowly and tapped the nape of the big Australian's neck. He was measuring the distance. The Aussie moaned softly as he felt the blade. The observer felt sick. 'Get on with it, you sadistic bastard,' he whispered to himself.

The Jap officer did. He gave a great grunt, clearly audible in the deathly silence which had now descended upon the dusty quayside. The blade flashed in the sun. It hissed down. There was an audible crunch as the sword smashed through the bone. Next moment blood spurted up in a bright red arc. The Australian's head, complete with old slouch hat, tumbled to the dirt. 'Holy mother of God,' his comrade moaned. 'Holy mother—'

His words were cut off the next moment. This time the executioner did not need to measure the distance. The cruel blade whistled down. *Crunch . . . crack . . .* and the other Australian's head rolled into the dust, leaving his corpse upright, blood welling up from his neck and then dribbling down his uniform in a red gore fountain . . .

That was the start. The officer yelled, '*Banzai . . . banzai*!' As he wiped the blade of his precious sword clean of blood on the shirt of the second dead Australian, his soldiers went wild. It was as if they had been seized by a primitive atavistic bloodlust. Bayonets flashed. Bayonets stabbed into soft flesh. Rifle butts slammed down on the heads of the Chinese women. Abruptly everything was bloody chaos and savage carnage. Scream after scream rang out. It didn't stop the soldiers. Indeed, it seemed to increase their primeval cruelty.

One of the Japs, perhaps weary of killing, tied a cord

around the severed heads of the two Australian soldiers and, before hauling them up to the overhead tramway cable, stuck lighted cigarettes in the dead men's gaping mouths. Now the two heads hung there, dripping blood from eyes and ears, quietly smoking away.

Another now arranged a dead coolie, very dark-skinned, so he might have been an Indian, the watching observer thought, trying to fight back the hot vomit in his throat, which threatened to choke him at any moment. Someone had split the victim from his shaven skull to his pubes. Now the blood-crazed Jap pulled the corpse further apart and in that purple case of the dead body he was arranging flowers in the Oriental fashion in a kind of sick, macabre wreath.

That was the final straw for the man with the rusty Raleigh bike. Choking back his vomit, he moved away, bowing all the while in case one of the Japanese still carrying out their dreadful slaughter might come running to bayonet him for his act of disrespect – leaving before he had been told he could do so.

But the Nips were too intent on their ghastly task to notice the skinny coolie, who was somehow too big for the usual native of his class. All the same he was glad of his only other piece of clothing – the rising-sun armband that indicated he was approved by the Japanese military government or, inferior coolie that he was, he had some Japanese blood running in his veins. Any marauding Nip would think twice about killing him out of hand.

With a furtive look to left and right to check whether he was being observed – he wasn't – he turned into the overgrown garden of one of the big European-style houses that had been burned out and abandoned during the Japanese bombing raids on Singapore back in December 1941. He had been here before. He knew his way about.

Still he wasted no time. The 'Kemptai', the Japanese secret police, were everywhere – and they were clever. They would pinpoint abandoned buildings like this one as an ideal hiding place for insurgents, saboteurs – *spies*, as he was.

He pushed aside one of the ant-eaten doors, hanging from its rusting hinges. He thrust the bike inside the passage beyond. There was an alarmed rustling. For a moment his heart ceased beating. Then he realized the noise had been made by rats, which infested such buildings searching for food – growing ever scarcer in Singapore, even for rats. 'Fucking rats . . .' he cursed and then added for good measure, 'And fuckin' Japs too!'

Then he forgot both the rodents and their two-legged human equivalents and got down to the urgent business of the day: the reason for his having risked his life here in occupied Singapore ever since the 'fucking Japs' had taken the so-called 'Gibraltar of the East'.

Hastily he dipped his fingers into the hollow frame tubing of the old Raleigh cycle. Bit by bit he brought out the parts of the high-speed transmitter. He noticed as he did so that his hands trembled slightly. But that was to be expected, he told himself as he moved quickly and expertly. If he were caught, the Japs wouldn't simply execute him. They would torture him at length and with every cruel refinement for extracting the maximum pain known to the Oriental mind till they had gotten every last bit of information out of his battered, agony-ridden body. That idea would make the bravest man tremble and he knew he wasn't the world's bravest.

He dismissed his fears. With a last movement, he slung the wire aerial over the top of the ruined door and raised his finger over the morse key. What he would do in a minute always required a deliberate act of will power.

Once he started, he knew that the Kemptai listening posts and camouflaged detector vans would go into action immediately. If they located him before he'd finished his signal and was on his way again, he'd be a dead duck. Hence it took the same sort of courage as his old Dad had needed to go over the top at Gallipoli in the old war and charge Johnny Turk. He took a deep breath like a champion about to jump off the high board in some spectacular dive and pressed his forefinger down on the key. He was in business.

'*Nips executed approx 100 civvies today . . . Two Aussie soldiers, too . . . No identity. Poor bastards . . . They suspect nothing . . . end.*'

Five minutes later he had disappeared into the teeming slums of the great port. Behind him he left the two heads of the executed Australians swinging slowly back and forth in the breeze, still dripping their blood on to the scene of the massacre below . . .

Book One

A Plan of Revenge

One

C olonel Lyn, his face deeply bronzed still from the daring secret raid, shivered slightly in the chill wind coming off the Solent. He was cold. It had come as a slight shock to him when he had arrived back in a bomb-shattered, grey London to realise just how cold the Old Country was after months in the Far East. Still, cold or not, the colonel was not a man to be hurried. He took his time, while the brigadier with the clipped moustache and brisk manner tut-tutted as if he couldn't get back to the War Office or perhaps his London club quick enough.

Over the quayside next to the big grey submarine, a three-striper in a faded blue jersey was hammering at a rusty sprocket, woefully singing the popular ditty of that summer: 'You'll get no promotion this side of the ocean, so cheer up my lads, bless 'em all . . . Bless 'em all, the long and the short and the tall . . .' The brigadier, obviously growing irate at the delay in the day's timetable, cupped his hands around his mouth and shouted, 'I say, you sailor . . . can't you put a sock in it? We can't hear ourselves ruddy well think up here.'

Colonel Lyn grinned as the sailor jumped to his feet, the stanchion clattering to the cobbles, as if he had just been given a jab with a red-hot poker, and, springing to attention, yelled back, 'Yessir . . . I mean, no, sir.

Singing to be stopped at once, *sir*!' Thereupon he swung the brigadier a tremendous salute.

Colonel Lyn grinned and the assembled officers of the naval conducting party tittered. Even the 'Druid', Lyn's sombre-faced Welsh batman, allowed himself a weak smile. The brigadier, for his part, shook his head as if he never ceased to wonder at the thick-headed foolishness of the average British serviceman. 'Well Lyn,' he barked, breath fogging on the cold air. 'What do you think?' He indicated the long sinister shape of the big sub.

Lyn, never one to be impressed by armchair warriors like the brigadier, who gave the orders, but weren't the ones who got their arses shot off in battle, said simply, 'She'll do, sir . . . Thank you.' He turned to the naval officers, all young men from the submarine service, and added, 'And thank you, too, gentlemen.'

The brigadier didn't waste any further time. 'Now then, Lyn, before our sexual appendages freeze off in this bloody wind, I want to show you something else. It might be more important in any future ops than the sub itself.' He nodded to the nearest naval officer. 'Will you do the honours, Commander?' It was at that moment that Brigadier Harvey Jenkins-Penfold caught sight of the Druid, with his doleful chapel face and ill-fitting battledress, devoid of any medal ribbons and adorned with the blood-red flash of the Royal Army Medical Corps.

He frowned and snapped, 'Who the devil is that, Lyn? I mean . . . the chap's a private soldier in . . . Medical Corps!'

Lyn's tough bronzed face broke into a wintry smile. He told himself that Private Ap Jones, known to his comrades of the X Commando as 'Holy Joe' and more often, because he was Welsh, as 'Druid', did look out of place here among these high-ranking officers, viewing the latest weapons for the war in the Far East. 'It's my batman, sir,' he answered, hoping that the Druid wouldn't open his mouth and say something. With that sing-song doleful voice of his, heavy with the sombre accents of the valleys, he'd raise the brigadier's blood pressure even higher. 'He goes with me everywhere, sir. Very fine man. Brave soldier.'

'Hm,' the brigadier sniffed, apparently satisfied, while the Druid looked puzzled and morose, both at the same time.

Behind the brigadier the lieutenant commander shrilled three blasts on a whistle hanging from a brilliant white card around his neck. A hundred yards or so away, the signalman started to wag his flags at once. Lyn tensed, his batman forgotten now, as he waited to see what surprise the SOE* brigadier was going to attempt to pull on him now.

For a few moments nothing happened. Then Lyn, his ears trained to catch the faintest sound by months of jungle training in guerrilla warfare, heard it. A faint mechanical hum. He strained harder. Yes, there it was. But it was not mechanical; it sounded more like the soft noise given off by an electric generator.

'Here they come, sir,' the lieutenant commander announced.

As one the party thrust up their binoculars and focused on the grey choppy water to their immediate front. For a second Lyn couldn't quite make out what the dark object was, skimming across the surface of the gleaming, calibrated glass of his field glasses.

Then he had it. He gasped slightly. It was some sort

*Special Operations Executive, a wartime secret intelligence and sabotage unit of the British Forces.

of elongated canoe-like object. But the man in the rubber
frogman's suit sitting in it was not using his paddle. The
canoe was seemingly moving of its own volition.

The brigadier had obviously heard the hard-faced commando colonel's little gasp, for he said in that hearty
manner of his kind, 'Caught you with your britches
down, what, Lyn . . . Never seen anything like it before,
I'll wager, what?'

'No sir,' Lyn confessed, not taking his glasses off
the first canoe-like object, which was being followed
by another, which, too seemed to skim the surface of
the water effortlessly, moving at what he guessed was
five knots. 'I must say that I haven't.'

Standing behind the officers, the Druid watched the
two objects getting ever closer and told himself, as if
it had come to him with the 100 per cent clarity of a
sudden vision, 'Trouble, boy bach . . . Real trouble is
on the way.' Little did the diminutive Welshman with
the swarthy features of a true Celt know just then how
right he was . . .

They stood or squatted on shooting sticks at the shel-
tered edge of the quay, drinking scalding hot tea laced
with a generous portion of naval rum. Above their heads
around Southsea, the fat silver barrage balloons swayed
back and forth like elephants about to go on the rampage.
Further off, red and white tracer zipped into the sky in
a lethal morse, trying to hit one of the new German
tip-and-run raiders which was trying to slip in under
the coastal defences and drop a couple of bombs on
some unfortunate coastal town. The officers didn't seem
to notice. Their attention was concentrated totally on the
two boats drawn up in the lee of the sea wall while the
SOE brigadier lectured them.

'Officially they're called the Mark II Boom Patrol

Boats,' he said. 'That's what Vospers, the engineers, call 'em. Our chaps who have been trying them out call them "Sleeping Beauties". Rather a good name, don't you think?' He beamed at Lyn. But the latter didn't respond. His gaze was fixed on the two top-secret craft, which he had already realized could be used underwater or just above the surface. Ideal for an attack on enemy shipping. At the back of his brain, a harsh little voice rasped, as if in warning, 'You've done it before, Ivan, and got away with it. Do you ruddy well think you'll get away with it a second time, even if you have these ruddy new toys?' Lyn ignored the warning voice and continued to listen, while at the same time he wondered how the two craft had achieved that tremendous 5-knot speed without the two crewmembers appearing to use their paddle. What was the secret of these – er – Sleeping Beauties?

It was now that the brigadier enlightened him. 'They're powered,' he announced, 'by an electric motor, so that in any beach assault, commando op, sabotage operation or the like, they can be launched well off shore – seven to ten kilometres or more. No one,' he ended proudly, as if he personally had done the job, 'has done this before, not even the Eyeties, and they have been the leaders and pioneers in these special craft, as everyone knows.'

Although Lyn, the big soldier and now commando working for SOE, was not accustomed to revealing his feelings, he couldn't quite repress a soft whistle at the brigadier's revelation. He knew immediately what this new development meant. A sub could stand well off shore out of the enemy's reach – for the Royal Navy didn't like endangering its precious subs on commando operations – and launch the Sleeping Beauties. That was one plus point. Another in favour of the new craft was that they could stooge around picking the most likely spot to land on the enemy coast, while the electric motors did the hard work and the crew could save their strength for the dangerous job to come. 'Something like this could change the whole face of combined ops, sir,' he said aloud.

'Exactly, Lyn.' The brigadier grinned, his face suddenly a beetroot red from the fierce naval rum. Behind him the Druid shook his head mournfully. He could see the brigadier was yet another addicted to the demon drink. There were too many of them like it in the Army. It would have been better if they'd all been sent to the chapel on a Sunday. He shook his head again, as if he simply couldn't understand this corrupt world he now found himself in.

'I mean,' the brigadier continued, 'the Sleeping Beauties have got everything going for them. They give the subs a better chance of survival. They are such good boats they can survive two- to three-metre waves in a Force Three blow and under power they make less disturbance than the usual paddled canoe. They're small enough to dodge a sonar sweep and are almost invisible to the human eye on the surface, especially at dawn and dusk.' He drained the rest of his rum and coughed, eyes sparkling suddenly with the powerful alcohol. 'Why, the Sleeping Beauty, Lyn, is a war-winning weapon in our particular field of endeavour, what.'

Lyn, although he disliked armchair warriors of the brigadier's type intensely, was forced to agree with him. For once, the SOE, full of crack-pot inventors – of guns that fired round corners, pieces of horse shit that turned out to be mines and the like – had come up with something that really worked. 'Looks like it, sir,' he conceded, but not too enthusiastically. He didn't want to encourage people like the brigadier. As he had warned his friend and adjutant, Captain 'Pongo' O'Dare, just before the briefing, 'Never encourage those staff wallahs, Pongo.

It goes to their heads and you know what happens then? They—'

But Pongo, a giant of Irish extraction who, prior to the war, had played rugger for the army, carrying the ball in his big paw as if it were a kids' table-tennis ball, had beaten him to it: '—Then proceed to plan to have our ruddy heads shot off.'

Now, as he remembered this warning while still staring with unconcealed admiration at the two Sleeping Beauties down below, he wondered whether they meant that the SOE had a new op for him. Why else should the brigadier bring him all the way from London to see them? Indeed, why had he been summoned home from Australia so hastily after the success of his last op? Was that hurried journey across half the world connected with these new craft? Somehow he suspected it was.

Down below, the first boat was preparing to move out to sea again. The commando in it, whom the brigadier called the 'pilot', lay back like some pre-war Grand Prix racing driver. He stretched his legs to their fullest extent, fingers around the handgrips on the joystick. Slowly he eased the stick forward. There was the soft sharp hiss of compressed air. Gradually the Sleeping Beauty began to submerge. Carefully the pilot trimmed the craft with the hand pump for the buoyancy tanks. She righted herself. Satisfied, the pilot switched on the engine. It started immediately. Slowly and carefully the Sleeping Beauty began to nose its way just below the ripple of the wavelets. It had been a perfect start. If Lyn had been an emotional man, given to displaying his feelings, he might have exclaimed like his Aussie commandos would have, 'She's a flaming beaut – Sleeping Beauty!' But he wasn't, at least not to strangers. Instead he was a tough ex-Gordon Highlander, a member of a dour Scottish regiment, not given to emotion save when they had had a dram or perhaps even more than one. So he contented himself with a direct question. 'What's the op, sir?'

But before the brigadier – who was beaming now that he realized he was not going to be forced into talking Lyn into the new action – could answer, Captain Pongo O'Dare came charging up as if he were back on the field at Twickenham, crying at the top of his voice, '*Signal, sir . . . signal, sir . . . All the way from Aussie . . .*'

Two

A high silver crescent moon had hung over Singapore as they had crept by the Straits of Johor. It had cast its spectral light over the still water. To the canoeists it seemed that anyone on the Sarangoon Road leading to the Singapore Town area should have spotted them without trying. But the Japs must have been asleep that night. No one did. So they moved on, the only sign of their presence, as they passed the Jap lookout posts, their soft white wakes.

Colonel Lyn shivered a little. It wasn't the cold. The tropical air was still warm from the humid heat of the day. It was the thought of what the little raiding team, which had travelled all the way from Sydney in faraway Australia for this bold, first-time attack on the Japs, would soon face: the minefield and the boom protecting the enemy shipping packed inside Singapore's harbour. One wrong move, the slightest slip-up, and he knew all hell would break loose. Thereafter they would not have a cat's chance in hell of escaping back to the waiting sub, which had brought them this far for the first commando raid ever launched in the Far East.

The minutes passed in leaden tension. Every time a light flashed on the island, Lyn caught his breath. Had they been discovered? They hadn't. Perhaps it was the light of some drunken Jap officer who had forgotten to black out the headlights of his car, looted when Singapore had surrendered a few months before. Even as he thought about it, Lyn felt the shiver of disgrace course down his spine. What a bloody mess that had been! The soldiers of the King-Emperor surrendering to half their number of bandy-legged, four-eyed Nips, who were supposed not even to have been able to shoot straight. Well, with a bit of luck, they'd start getting their own back this night.

Now, by straining their eyes, the raiders could just make out the dimmed-out lights of the waterfront. The Japs obviously weren't taking the blackout too seriously. Perhaps they had won so many easy victories since December 7th, 1941, that they had lost all their fears that the Anglo-American white devils might strike back. All to the good, he told himself, now able to pick out the stark black silhouettes of the numerous ships outlined by the lights. He licked his cracked, parched lips as if he were hungry. Plenty of tempting targets there, he whispered to himself.

'Skipper.' It was Pongo, who was the lead paddler.

'Yes?'

'We're on the edge of the minefield.'

'How?'

'Buoy to portside. Painted red as far as I can make out.'

Lyn shot a look in that direction, eyes screwed up in order to see better. 'Yes,' he agreed. 'Marker buoy. You're right. Slow ahead it is.'

'Bleeding very exceedingly slow,' his old comrade whispered back.

They commenced paddling again. Now Lyn could feel his hands suddenly wet and greasy with sweat. Beads of it coursed down his spine. His breath was coming quick and sharp. Tension. He had to get a bloody grip of himself.

Still, it was damnably difficult. Perhaps only a mere foot or so beneath the paper-thin hull of their little craft, some deadly ball of high explosive was waiting patiently to blow them to kingdom come. They had to concentrate or else . . .

Now the two of them strained their eyes in the gloom for the tell-tale sign of impending danger: the horn of a tethered mine bobbing up and down in the wavelets, waiting for them to run into it, and all the time they were running ever closer to the Jap ships. There, there would be lookouts pacing the decks. If the mines didn't get them, Lyn told himself, then the bloody Nips—

'*Mine!*' Pongo's whispered warning cut into his thoughts like the blade of a sharp knife.

'Where?'

'Starboard . . . Got it?'

'Yes, got it.' Lyn could hardly recognize his own voice. 'Stop paddling for half a mo.' Pongo didn't hesitate. He stopped at once. There could be only one skipper in a situation like this.

Now they drifted towards the deadly pronged metal ball. Lyn took a deep breath. Gingerly, trying not to rock the craft and cause any disturbance in the water, he started to lean over the side. Slowly, very slowly, he reached out with both hands. Suddenly they touched the hard wet metal of the horn.

Lyn swallowed hard. It was now or never. He started to push. He slipped. Just in time he bit back the cry of alarm. The nearest Jap ship was only a hundred yards or so away now. He tried again. This time, balancing the best he could, in danger of falling into the water at any time, he got a firmer hold. 'Pongo,' he croaked. 'Start up again.'

'Yes, skipper.' Pongo's voice was as strained as his. Very delicately, he dipped his paddle into the water. The

25

little craft began to move. His shoulder muscles burning like fire now with the pain and strain, Lyn commenced pushing the wet slippery surface of the mine. Behind them the second canoe started to follow, keeping exactly in their wake.

Time passed leadenly. Later it would seem to Lyn as if he had been pushing the bloody Jap mine for an eternity. In reality it was probably only seconds. Then the mine was slipping away from beneath his fingers and, with a great sobbing sigh of relief, he righted himself and, regaining his balance, he watched as it slipped away into the gloom, his heart beating furiously.

But there was no time now to waste on enjoying his sense of relief that they were through the minefield. Ahead of them the dark hulls of the Jap ships anchored in Singapore harbour were looming up on all sides. They had to get to work. This was, after all, the reason for their thousand-odd mile journey from Australia. They would have to do the maximum damage. What ships should they choose?

Now they were right inside of the Japs. The water stank of diesel. But the smell of the rancid spices the Japs used on their rice balls was even stronger. But even as Lyn wrinkled his nose in disgust at the stench, he knew they had struck lucky. That stench indicated that somewhere there were a lot of Japs indulging themselves in their filthy grub. And that could indicate one thing and one thing only. A Jap naval vessel with a big crew on board, or even an Imperial Army troopship. What a prize that would be – to sink a troopship filled with hundreds of those Nip infantrymen who had originally defeated the British in Singapore so shamefully. What an admirable revenge that would be!

Five minutes passed as the two canoes spread out but

kept sight of each other. The tension was electric. Once they heard the throbbing and swish of some picket boat. Hurriedly they edged into the shadow of the nearest ships. But whatever the craft was, it passed without noticing them.

Then Lyn had his first target. He was alerted to her size by the steaming roar from her sewage outflow as the stinking waste poured from a height into the harbour. 'Pongo, this is number one,' he whispered urgently, as the big ex-rugby player back-paddled.

Pongo whispered his understanding and held the canoe steady now, as the CO leaned over the side carefully. With both his hands free he clamped the mine to the ship's hull, just below the waterline. It made a noise as the magnet attached to the steel hull. But the water muffled the sound somewhat. All the same, Lyn found his hands were trembling badly afterwards. For he knew now, he wouldn't live more than five minutes or so if the Nips cottoned on to his presence here in the middle of Singapore harbour at this time of the night.

Meanwhile the second canoe, with the Druid as lead paddler, was weaving in and out of the silent hulks almost noiselessly, seeking the best targets for the precious limpets, the commandos keeping a weather eye out for Jap sentries and the like. They had all done this sort of thing a dozen times in training and felt they could carry it out with their eyes shut. But just like the CO and Pongo O'Dare, they too realized this was the real thing. They were striking back for the first time from the sea, and the Japs would exact a terrible penalty for their temerity in doing so, if they were caught.

Another ten minutes passed in electric tension. By now all of them were streaming with sweat, their nerves frayed and jumpy. But still there had been no sudden shout of

27

alarm, rage, fear, which would herald the fact that they had been spotted. Japan's most important harbour in the Far East was seemingly locked in a dreamless sleep.

Hastily Lyn looked at the remaining limpets and made his decision. There were two, perhaps three, of them left in the darkness at the bottom of the canoe, straddled by Pongo's big feet. If he could find a suitable target, he'd use all three of them on it. It was no use hanging around much longer. Despite the apparent calm of the harbour, they'd be bound to be discovered in the end. Why waste the whole bold operation for the sake of destroying more targets? He made up his mind. He'd head for what he thought – and hoped fervently – was a trooper some hundred yards away. Even in the gloom, he could see the occasional flurry of white steam coming from its superstructure. That could indicate that not just the crew were aboard, but also plenty of other Japs, and hopefully they were soldiers.

Swiftly he whispered his instructions to Pongo. He nodded his understanding in the same instant that the Druid drew up beside them and said in a husky voice that trembled slightly with tension, 'Used all my limpets, sir.'

'Follow us,' Lyn ordered and started paddling right away. There was no time to be lost. The stars had vanished now. To the east, the sky was beginning to grow a dull ugly white. It indicated that dawn was not far off, and when dawn came in the Far East, Lyn knew, it came with dramatic suddenness, illuminating everything in its fierce yellow tropical light. Time was running out.

They came closer to the big Japanese ship now. Lyn could smell it before he could make out its full outline. It stank of stable, that smell he remembered from his country youth: a mixture of horse shit and the warm comfortable sweaty odour of horses nuzzling their halters and shuffling their feet in anticipation of the new day. The big ship was obviously carrying an Imperial Army cavalry squadron. His heart leapt at the thought of the damage he might do to it, though he didn't like to think of how the horses might suffer in the subsequent explosion and fire. The Japanese had absolutely no regard for human life. He guessed, therefore, they wouldn't give a tinker's damn about their mounts. He dismissed the horrifying thought.

Now, while Pongo back-paddled and the Druid in his boat did the same, keeping a little way off the hull so that he and the other commando could watch the Japanese ship's upper deck and superstructure for any suspicious movement, Lyn began to attach the first mine. He had picked a spot midships and just beneath the Plimsoll line. With a bit of luck, when the limpet exploded, it might break the trooper's back.

Finished, he nodded. Pongo needed no further instruction. They had been well trained to carry out the mine-fixing operation without orders. They glided silently the length of the hull, making so little noise that Lyn could hear the shuffle and sniggering of the horses in their stalls next to the waterline. He frowned, but said nothing. He concentrated on finding the location of the engine room. He felt the steel plating. Sure enough it was getting hotter. He was approaching the engines. One of them was obviously being kept going to supply the heating and light for cooking. He was almost there. Behind him Pongo lifted up the heavy limpet, as if it was a kids' toy.

It was then that it happened – the thing Lyn and the rest had feared ever since they had left the sub and set out on this bold mission. With dramatic, frightening suddenness, a searchlight cut the pre-dawn gloom. Abruptly a hard white beam barred their way and was now beginning to come towards them. The worst had happened!

Three

The four canoeists froze.

Lyn felt his heart thumping like a trip hammer. The sound seemed deafening. Behind him, Pongo moved. Slowly, very slowly, he reached for his Sten gun. It was the latest model and was fitted with a silencer. What exactly the big Irishman was going to do with it, he didn't know. But he knew he was not going to be taken without a fight. Slowly, very slowly, that frightening beam of light came ever closer to them.

The Druid started to pray. It was the kind of simple plaintive prayer they always used in the chapel on the hill next to the slag heap in the rainswept valley in which he had been born. It had none of the eloquence of the C. of E. prayers he had been accustomed to in the Army, but it comforted him. As always, prayer drove out the devils, even the lecherous sexual ones, that so often tormented him on his sleepless nights. Now the beam was almost upon them.

Lyn felt a cold bead of sweat trickle slowly down the small of his back. It was now or never. Here it came. The icy white beam swept their bent heads. Later Lyn could have sworn that it was red-hot and actually burned the back of his head, but of course he knew that was a foolishness; it was simply a matter of his nerves running away with him. But that was later.

Nothing happened!

Slowly the searchlight passed over them and continued its progress over the still waters of the great anchorage. For what seemed an eternity none of them moved. It was as if they were characters in a third-rate melodrama, frozen into position in the last moment of the final scene, waiting for the hoped-for burst of applause.

Pongo croaked. 'Bugger that for a tale o' soldiers, Colonel. But we've done—'

He never finished the sentence. Up above on the top deck of the troopship, if that was what she was, a hoarse voice cried, '*Hi!*' A moment later the challenge rang out and Lyn knew with a dreadful sinking feeling that they had been spotted after all.

'I nearly shat myself,' Pongo said afterwards. Now he reacted instinctively. He raised the Sten gun and pressed the trigger. At that distance he couldn't miss, even with the notoriously poor Sten. The weapon jerked in his big paws. There was the abrupt whiff of burned cordite. Empty cartridge cases splattered into the water.

Up above there was a shrill scream of almost unbearable agony. It was followed by the clatter of a rifle falling to the steel deck plates. Next moment, the solid thud of the sailor or whoever the Jap was following suit. Thereafter there was a loud echoing silence that seemed to the tense men below almost deafening, interspersed by soft moans.

Lyn cursed. He knew what he had to do, but he was rooted to the spot, it seemed, not wanting to do it. In the end, after what felt like an age, he said to Pongo, 'I'm going to have to get that slant-eyed bugger.' He pointed upwards to where the Japanese lookout presumably lay on the deck.

'Must you, Ivan?' Pongo asked in a hushed whisper. 'Can't we leave him?'

31

'No, it will be a dead giveaway. If we can manage it, we don't want to give 'em any clue who was here and how this all happened.' He didn't wait for Pongo to object any further. 'Give me your toggle – at the double now,' he added sharply when Pongo seemed reluctant to give him the length of rope that each commando carried tied round his waist.

Swiftly he tied his own and Pongo's toggles together, giving him a fairly sizeable rope. Twirling it around his head he launched it upwards. There was the faint click of the metal toggle 'eye' catching on to something. Swiftly he gave the rope his full weight. It held. He wasted no more time. Bracing himself with both feet against the wet hull, he started to climb upwards while, below, the Druid, who worshipped the CO like one of the forbidding Gods of his chapel, prayed fervently that Lyn would make it without being discovered.

Hand over hand, Lyn went up the steep slippery steel side of the ship with professional ease, yet knowing that he could be discovered at any moment. He reached the lower deck. Somewhere there was the faint sound of snoring. He nodded his approval. He hoped that the whole of the ship's crew was similarly engaged. Next instant a soft moan indicated that someone was not sleeping. It was the wounded man somewhere directly above his head. 'Balls,' he cursed to himself and moved on immediately.

He found the little Japanese sailor writhing with his knees tucked up into his stomach, rocking back and forth in what he knew from the past was mortal agony. The sailor was dying. In fact, Lyn guessed from the amount of blood around him that the Japanese had only a matter of minutes, perhaps half an hour at the most, to live. He touched him gingerly. The Japanese turned round. He caught a glimpse of the Jap's face. It was almost hairless – he was hardly more than a boy. For a moment the dying Jap's eyes opened and there was a sudden look of hope in them. He thought he was being saved. Lyn bit his bottom lip. He felt sorry for the kid. Next instant he told himself the dying Jap was the enemy. Kid or no kid, he was probably as cruel as the rest of his compatriots. He knew they couldn't help it. They were trained by their superiors to be cruel to one another and even more so to their prisoners. Lyn had had his bellyful of Jap cruelty to helpless POWs. There was no excuse for it, try as he might to find one.

Roughly he gathered the boy up in his brawny arms. The Jap moaned and he felt his hands abruptly wet with warm blood. The kid was going too fast. Walking on the tips of his toes, he slipped to the companionway. Hurriedly he advanced down to the next deck. Now his nostrils were assailed by the pungent odour of oriental cooking. Down below in the galleys, the cooks were beginning to prepare breakfast. He had to get himself and his prisoner over the side at once. Every second counted. He could be discovered at any moment now.

Sweating hard, cursing to himself as if he were a very angry man, he lugged the dying man to the next deck. The Jap kid was making terrible gurgling sounds deep in his throat. Lyn had seen enough mortally wounded men; he knew the kid was in his death throes. But that didn't concern him. He paused at the railing and drew a deep breath. This was telling on him. He had to lighten his load soon. After all, it was going to be a long haul back to the waiting submarine.

Abruptly his weariness vanished. Someone was coming up along the deck. He could distinctly hear the clump-clump of the wooden clog-like sandals some Japs wore.

He pressed the dying boy to him as if they were hot-blooded lovers and retreated deeper into the shadows. The hard sound of the wooden-soled shoes on the rusting steel of the deck came ever closer. He freed one hand gingerly. Slowly, very slowly, he reached for his knife. Pressed close to him, the Jap was still bleeding but the terrible gurgling noises ceased. Was he dead? Lyn hoped he was. If he was not, the kid might well betray—

Suddenly the noise of the wooden clogs ceased. Lyn tensed. He felt his big shoulder muscles clench. His hand tightened on the knife, his palm wet with sweat and blood. He waited. Someone close by – it had to be the Jap in the clogs – farted pleasurably. A moment later the noise was followed by a stream of water falling to the sea below. Lyn swallowed hard and relaxed a little. Someone had not risked going to the latrines, probably earth privies in the Japanese fashion – or perhaps he was just too lazy – and he had come on deck to urinate over the side.

The stream of urine seemed to go on for ever. But finally it was over and there was the clump-clump sound of the man in the clogs returning back to his quarters. Lyn gave him ten seconds, counting them off slowly and carefully under his breath. Then, getting a tighter hold of the kid, who he thought was probably dead now, he dragged him to the rail. He grunted, heaved and let the body go. It struck the water below. It went under. Next moment he heard the soft stroke of Pongo's paddle. He had spotted the body as it had returned to the surface in a flurry of phosphorescence and was heading straight for it.

Lyn gave a sigh of relief. A second later, he too was clambering down the rope to the waiting craft. Operation Jaywick was almost over . . .

*　　*　　*

They were almost exhausted as the submarine began to surface, shedding water like some great metallic whale. It had been a hell of a trip, especially towing the dead Japanese behind them with the aid of their toggles. It had made it difficult to keep the Druid's canoe on course and entailed hard paddling against the sea current as they got out of the harbour and into the open ocean. Indeed, dedicated chapel-goer that he was, the swarthy Welshman surprised the Aussie commando who crewed the little canoe with him by twice uttering an angry 'Blast!' Once he even exclaimed, 'Ruddy hard work this, Blue.'

If the Aussie had not been knackered himself, he would have remarked on this outburst of profanity by the man the Australian contingent called 'Ruddy Old Holy Joe' or 'Bloody Bible Thumper'. But he was too exhausted to do so and he, too, leaned over his paddle, gasping and hoping that once the sub had surfaced, the crew would treat him to a big cup of grog. At the moment that was the only thing in the world that 'Blue' desired. He'd even give up a naked blonde with tits like melons for a good honest slug of Navy rum.

Half an hour later they were recovered somewhat and Lyn and Pongo were already deep in conversation with the young skipper of the submarine as the crew prepared to dive once more, ready for the long voyage back to Sydney. On the deck lay sprawled the dead body of the Japanese boy. Every now and again, the busy deckhands stepped over the Jap. Some of them, the old sweats, didn't seem even to notice him. Others, the younger ratings, looked down at the corpse, as if they felt some sort of sympathy with him, and once Pongo heard one of them say, 'Why don't they bury the poor little sod. It ain't right to leave him just like that, poor Jap perisher.'

Pongo shook his head in mock wonder. Once again he

asked himself why the English couldn't be real haters. In war you had to hate your enemies with a passion. But that seemed damnably difficult for a lot of Englishmen.

'Now, what's the drill?' the sub commander asked. 'We get rid of the corpse—'

'I'll take care of stripping him,' Lyn cut in, as if he were in a great hurry now.

The young skipper looked puzzled, but didn't comment. 'We're to move in, of course, and report on the success of the limpets.'

'Naturally,' Lyn responded. 'But I'm hoping now that the Japs won't guess their shipping has been sabotaged from the sea.' His face was suddenly thoughtful, as if other ideas were beginning to uncoil like deadly serpents inside of his active imagination. 'That's why I want to get rid of the body – naked – out here. In a way, even though he's snuffed it, he is the only evidence that we've been here.'

'But why worry?' Pongo cut in, puzzled too.

'I'll tell you later.' Lyn brushed aside his old friend's question impatiently. 'The fewer who know about what I have in mind the better.' He turned to the Druid. 'I'm going to strip the body. I want you to view it when I've finished. I want you to tell me what you think of it, just in case it ends up in the hands of the enemy. Is that clear?'

'Sir,' the Druid replied, while next to him the big Aussie sniggered.

'Well in with the gentry, ain't yer, mate? Will yer say a frigging prayer for our yellow man?' He laughed maliciously.

But no one said a prayer for the dead boy. His naked body, bloody holes where Lyn personally had ripped out two of the Sten bullets so that the evidence of their presence here in enemy waters was removed, floated in the wake of the submarine as it prepared to dive. For a moment or two it bobbed up and down as the water was churned into a white fury by the screws of the sub. Then, as the vessel slid below the surface, it calmed down . . .

Far, far away on the horizon to the north, there was a sudden pale-red flickering in the morning sky. The first of the limpets had exploded and Lt Colonel Ivan Lyn, who now had only half a year to live, grinned in triumph as he peered through the periscope. The bold plan had worked. Without a single casualty and despite the lack of enthusiasm on the part of the Joint Allied Command back in Australia, he had pulled off the longest commando raid in history. Now the question was – could he do it again?

Down among the torpedoes, the bunks filled with snoring matelots and commandos, the Druid prayed.

Four

The three officers sat round the table in the wardroom, sipping their pink gins, while an attentive Druid, togged out in a borrowed white jacket, waited at the serving hatch for their instructions. They were in high good spirits. The new equipment that the authorities were now putting at the disposal of the SOE Commando, plus the startling message from Sydney, had charged them with new energy and enthusiasm after the hard cold day on the seafront. Indeed, the Druid didn't like the situation one bit. He felt his beloved colonel was over-indulging, as the Brigadier and Captain O'Dare were too. They'd already gone through one bottle of the pink gin and were now well into their second of the 'demon' drink, and everyone knew that drink had ruined more than one good officer. He said a little prayer that Colonel Lyn would cease now, so that he could give him a nice hot supper of eggs (real ones and not powdered) and bacon and put him to bed so that he could get a good rest for the busy schedule that lay ahead of him on the morrow.

But the three officers, secreted in the comfy, smoke-filled atmosphere of the warm wardroom, seemed to be in no hurry to eat and sleep. Indeed, by the look of animation on their drink-reddened faces, it appeared that they might go on all night. The Druid looked at them severely, giving them the benefit of his most disapproving look, so that Pongo O'Dare guffawed and bellowed, 'Now, Druid, don't fill your pants, we're just having a mild celebration, you know. It's not as if we are in the last stages of the DTs or something.'

The brigadier, who had drunk his share of the Navy gin, agreed with, 'Typical Welsh, you know, miserable buggers, can't enjoy anything themselves and don't want anyone else to do so either.' He shook his head in mock wonder, 'Ruddy Celtic temperament! Give me the bloody old bovine Anglo-Saxons any day of the week.'

Lyn took pity on his servant. It was bad enough that the poor bugger was ragged by his comrades of the SOE Commando. He ought to be protected from officers doing the same, especially when they were in their cups. Besides, he thought it might be better if, now that he was prepared to make his proposal, it weren't done in the presence of the other ranks, even one as loyal and trustworthy as the poor taunted Welshman. 'All right, old chap,' he said in his most kindly manner. 'That's enough for today. Go over to the cookhouse and get yourself something to eat. Have the rest of the evening off. I won't need you till reveille. The usual – a mug of tea and my shaving water.'

'What about a couple of aspirins, sir, as well?' Pongo butted in. 'Might need 'em.'

Lyn ignored the comment. Old Pongo was well away, he told himself. He was really hitting the pink gin. He waited till the Druid had refilled their glasses, clicked his heels together in a token of military respect and departed before he turned to the signal from Sydney which had come in completely out of the blue and in its way had thrown SOE plans for a new op against the Japs into confusion.

Once again he spread it out in front of his companions

and said, his voice a little thick with drink, 'You can see the Japs think that the thirty-five thousand tons of shipping we sank in Singapore last month went to the bottom as a result of local sabotage. They've arrested and killed a lot of Chinese, Malays and our own people on that count.' He frowned hard at the thought. 'They've had to pay the supreme penalty, according to our agent in Singapore, for what we did. Poor sods.'

'We've all got to make sacrifices for the sake of the Empire and the King Emperor,' the brigadier intoned solemnly, the ends of his waxed military moustache wet with gin and drooping a little now.

Lyn was about to say something highly unprofessional, but Pongo flashed him a warning – his second in command knew just how much the CO hated these headquarter types like the brigadier. Lyn took the warning and contented himself with a mumbled, 'I suppose.'

Pongo thought it was time for him to step in and he asked, 'I see that. But what has the fact that the Jap doesn't know that we carried out the op have to do with any new op we may carry out, sir?'

'*This*,' Lyn's voice was suddenly hard and thrusting. 'He doesn't know we came by sea to sabotage their vessels. After all, why should the Jap suspect we can sail so many hundreds of miles from Aussie or somewhere thereabouts to attack his Far Eastern harbours? No one has ever carried out commando-type raids that far before. So,' he concluded, 'we ought to be able to catch him with his knickers down yet again.'

'You mean, Lyn, do it again?' the brigadier breathed.

'Exactly, sir.'

'Perhaps Rangoon, Lyn?' the brigadier suggested. 'Churchill will like that. Rangoon, Singapore. He'll maintain the Japs have lost control of the whole long coastline.'

He grinned stupidly at the other two, as if he had just made a brilliant suggestion.

As tipsy as he was, Colonel Lyn was in no mood for playing games, especially with this chairborne warrior, who would be sitting pretty in Whitehall with his fancy dinners at his club, White's, with his nubile young ATS* mistress when, as he told his battleaxe of a wife, he had 'to work overtime in the War House, old thing'. They, on the other hand, would be risking their lives hundreds of miles from base, trying to outwit the Japs. 'No,' he said, iron in his voice abruptly. 'I don't think that should be our objective at all, sir.'

'Pray what should be your target then, Lyn?' The brigadier took another hefty drink of his pink gin.

'Singapore!'

'*Again?*' both Pongo and the brigadier exclaimed in wonder.

'Yes,' Lyn answered. 'That signal from Sydney confirms what I have been thinking ever since we completed Operation Jaywick. The Japs don't know we raided Singapore. If they did, they would have publicized the news in the press and radio and naturally they wouldn't have slaughtered those poor innocents. So I think they will *not* have strengthened or altered their sea defences at Singapore against a similar raid. Therefore, my suggestion is that we repeat the raid using these new Sleeping Beauties, making it a larger and more comprehensive attack.' He looked at the brigadier and added swiftly, as if he were giving the armchair warrior some sort of consolation prize. 'If the Singapore raid works out, we head down the coast for Rangoon and, before they

*Auxiliary Territorial Service, i.e. the women's branch of the Army.

41

can strengthen their coastal defences there, we launch our secondary attack.' He shrugged. 'Thereafter, I think we'll have outlived our usefulness as a strike force against major Jap targets. It'll be up to your SOE, Brigadier, to then think up other objectives for us.'

Pongo's Irish blood flared up. 'By God, what a damn good idea! We can cut down the training to a minimum. There's still plenty of our chaps in Aussie who went on the last job who'll go with us. They're old hands. They wouldn't need training. Hell, we could start almost immediately, once we get the gear and supplies together.'

Lyn nodded, though he wasn't so confident about the men still in Australia volunteering for another attack on Singapore. Missions like Jaywick put a hell of a strain on the men; and if they had heard, too, of the mass execution carried out by the Japs the previous month, well that wouldn't exactly fill them with enthusiasm for another attack on Singapore. But the tall, bronzed commando colonel kept his thoughts to himself and waited for the brigadier's reaction. For it would be the Whitehall warrior who would put the proposal forward to Lord Mountbatten's Far-Eastern Supreme Headquarters in Ceylon for approval. What did he think?

In the event, the brigadier was too far gone in his cups to think very much, though he looked suitably stern, forehead wrinkled, as if he were thinking hard. 'Well, Lyn, you have a point,' he said finally. 'I think I could sell the idea to Lord Louis with a bit of luck.' He took another drink.

'Good show, sir,' Pongo, his light-blue eyes blazing with that old fierce Irish fighting spirit, enthused.

'Yes sir, go ahead and *sell it*,' Lyn added cynically. But cynicism was wasted on the brigadier and Lyn told himself that the senior officer was already wondering what kind of gong the powers-that-be would give him if the op were a success.

Now they had agreed, they started to talk the op over. Pongo fetched another bottle of gin from the wardroom petty officer. Over in the barracks (for this particular naval ship was a land-locked one, which would never go to sea, but still the Royal Navy stuck to the old traditions) a marine bugler sounded lights out. The flushed, excited officers didn't notice. The Druid went 'home'. He had naturally avoided the noisy pubs and the importuning whores who were everywhere. Instead he had been to the local chapel and had said a few prayers with the minister, who, joy upon joy, had been a Welshman and felt the same disgust as he did at the way the troops were behaving. 'Boy, bach,' he had exclaimed, his thin pinched cheeks flushed with outrage, raising his skinny forefinger, as if giving one of his fire-and-brimstone sermons. 'There'll be a day of reckoning soon. Take my word for it.' To which the soldier had replied, tears in his eyes, 'Amen to that, Mr Oakley-Jones. Amen to that!'

Now he pressed his head to the closed wardroom door and was shocked again. They were still talking and from the animated manner in which they did so, he guessed they were all drunk. He shook his head sadly and went off to his own bunk, where he said quite a number of urgent prayers for the 'sinners'' souls, in particular, for that of his CO, who he could only believe had been led astray at some point of his military career or other. For everyone knew military life was more sinful than that of Sodom and Gomorrah in ancient times.

Despite the alcohol, Lyn still kept to the main purpose of his new plan, ensuring that the brigadier, who had removed his tie as well as his battledress blouse by now and who was leaning back in one of the battered wardroom chairs, his feet on the table, was still with him. For he knew just how these staff officers blew with the wind. Faced with Lord Mountbatten, as vain as they came and jealous of his reputation for success, the brigadier would waver at once if the Supreme Commander didn't like the plan. Then, Lyn knew from his year-long career as a commando leader in the Far East that he was not only fighting the Japanese, but also the Allied staff and, in particular, Lord Louis in his remote HQ in the luxury of Ceylon.

Lyn emphasized the need to use the new secret weapon – the Sleeping Beauty – in a large-scale op; how the Marines, the Commandos and the top-secret Special Boat Service, all units specially favoured by his Lordship, would give all the support they were able to in an operation of this kind. He stressed that they already had a nucleus of trained men so that, as Pongo had already pointed out, the operation could get underway almost at once. Finally he pointed out the morale-boosting factor. If this second raid on Singapore succeeded, and this time they wouldn't be able to keep it secret, the British public so used to hearing of one Japanese victory after another, would learn the tide was changing. The British Empire was striking back at long last.

As drunk as he was, the brigadier attempted to sit up at the mention of the Empire. 'By gad, Lyn, you're right,' he said thickly. 'Can't let the old Empire down, what.' He belched and looked more stupid than he usually did, while, behind his back, Pongo pretended to be playing an imaginary trumpet, red-flushed face suitably solemn. 'I think,' the brigadier continued with difficulty, 'we ought to give this operation a name that will stand out . . .

perhaps go down in history. You know what Mr Churchill is like. He's very keen on heroic names, things like that, for British military ops.' Again he hiccuped and Lyn thought for a minute he'd fall off his chair. He caught himself in time, however, and said, 'Think I'll have a drinkie.' He reached for the bottle and took a slug straight from its neck. His face went a puce colour. 'Jolly good,' he gasped, fighting for breath and lapsed into a glassy-eyed silence.

'Not heroic,' Lyn said. 'Defiant, dangerous, daring!' He rapped out the words with sudden chiselled precision, as if he had abruptly become very sober, which he wasn't. On a sudden impulse, he ripped open his shirt and bared his chest.

Pongo gave a gasp. 'I say, old chap,' he started. But his CO didn't give him time to finish. He bent his head to indicate the blazing yellow, black and white tattoo which covered his breast. '*Rimau*,' he interrupted. 'That's its name in Malay.'

Pongo stared at the snarling tiger's head, which some cunning native hand had tattooed on Lyn's chest when he had been stationed in the Malay Straits before the war. 'Bloody impressive,' he breathed. 'Not something you'd like to meet on a dark night, eh, old bean.'

'Exactly. Let's hope the Japs'll think the same, Pongo, for that's what we're going to call this new op – Operation Rimau!'

'Well, I'll be buggered,' Pongo snorted. 'Some moniker. But let's put it into English, shall we? Let's call it Operation Malay Tiger.'

Happily Colonel Lyn stretched out his hand and grasped that of his old comrade. 'Well, said, Pongo! That's what we'll call it. Operation Malay Tiger . . .'

Five minutes later, both were fast asleep, snoring loudly,

while the brigadier, very drunk, but no longer sleeping, stared intently at that fearsome tattoo in bewilderment, wondering where the devil he had landed this summer's night of 1943 . . .

Book Two

Nippon Plays a Hand

One

C olonel Tanaka of the Kemptai stared at the Eurasian girl's unconscious body. She lay on the table in the underground interrogation cellar. His policemen had strapped her down in such a way that her fine, pink-nippled breasts and the soft down of the Mound of Venus – in his romantic fashion he liked to think of the pubic bulge thus – were thrust up in an unnatural, but highly provocative manner. Indeed, he was so taken by her sexual attractiveness that he had forgotten the reason she was here. Lieutenant Kimura, his second in command, had brought her in for interrogation.

Leaning against the wall of the cellar, Lieutenant Kimura, tall for a Japanese, elegant and cynical, smoked and watched the little scene with hooded eyes. He knew Tanaka's problems and thought him a gross, perverted fool, who should have been pensioned off and sent back to Osaka, long ago. Still, he hadn't been, and so he, Kimura, had to live with him and his eternal perverted striving for sexual gratification. Still, the pervert had good connections to the Imperial Court and more importantly to General Tojo himself, the real ruler of Japan. So, he waited and smoked his cigarette and allowed his chief to play his silly little purposeless games. Naturally this one would never be one that Tanaka could win just like the rest.

49

Absently Tanaka stroked the thick blue-steel barrel of his American pistol. He always kept it close, though he was never in any danger. But the pistol seemed to give some sort of comfort, he knew not why. With his soft, pudgy, manicured hand, he stroked its hard power, little red eyes glued to the Eurasian girl's naked body.

She was beautiful – in spite of the cruel marks his torturers had left on her naked torso. She had a true athlete's body, like those of the American female athletes he had always admired in the pre-war newsreels imported from America. Her legs were long and muscular and very straight for a Eurasian. Her waist was small and tight, with the upper torso swelling out to those breasts with their erect pink nipples, as if she were sexually excited too. God, how he would have loved to suckle them slowly, very slowly, until he was ready for the other thing, which he dare not name even to himself. Unconsciously he rubbed the gun barrel more firmly.

The fat Japanese colonel licked his thick sensual lips. They were very dry. Now, after he had licked them, they gleamed a bright red against the dusky yellow of his skin. Watching him, Lieutenant Kimura thought he was like a pig. What a person to have to work with and report to. The man's brains were between his legs, he told himself, and even that thing wasn't working.

Kimura had arrested her and brought her here for immediate interrogation. But Colonel Tanaka had intervened; he often did when pretty women were arrested, especially if they were light-skinned like this Eurasian woman. He had called in his torturers, the muscular, sadistic ones whose creed was you could beat the truth out of any prisoner, if you worked at it long enough. As Sergeant Uchida was wont to boast, 'I can make even a mummy talk!' Systematically the Kemptai men had raped the woman, while the colonel watched, drooling the whole while.

They had thought it great fun, especially Sergeant Uchida. As Joshi, who was tall and came from one of Japan's northern islands, had slipped down his trousers to reveal he was already erect, his penis jutting out in front of him like the policeman's truncheon he carried, Uchida had sneered, 'You know what they say about tall men, don't you? They're like tall houses – the bottom floor is worst furnished!'

Joshi had frowned and after that hadn't enjoyed his few minutes with the Eurasian woman, bound and helpless, however much she might struggle and shriek on the table – pounding away at her as if he were doing it out of duty and not pleasure.

Colonel Tanaka had enjoyed it, however. Each stroke, each shriek, each animal grunt had excited him, but in the end, as he had rubbed the barrel of his revolver feverishly, Lieutenant Kimura knew it would result, for the fat colonel, in absolutely nothing. He was like a very old man who dozed the days away, thinking of his youth and his conquests of long before, which would never be repeated. Colonel Tanaka was totally, completely, unutterably *impotent*!

Tanaka waddled towards the woman. His hand holding the gun was shaking badly now. He ran his pig-like little eyes over her body. His heart started to beat rapidly. He searched every mound, beautiful hollow, wet dripping orifice. God . . . God . . . God, he whispered to himself fervently, so carried away by sexual excitement that he felt he might faint. Gingerly he touched her left breast, red and ripped with savage bites now. He shivered. His gross jowls trembled like puddings. He felt he was going mad. He pressed the revolver barrel, as if he might snap it in

51

two. He ran his hand across her stomach. He stopped at the
Mount of Venus. Below, her vulva gaped, red, swollen,
wet and ready. He hesitated. Dare he . . . Oh, God, dare
he? Why should he be cursed like this? In Singapore he
was all-powerful. He could do what he liked. Here he
could realize his wildest, craziest dreams. And yet . . .

Lieutenant Kimura had had enough of the fat voyeur.
He released his cigarette from its ivory holder. It dropped
to the floor. He stamped it out without looking down.
He crooked a finger at Sergeant Uchida, the show-off,
to pick up the butt. Uchida frowned. Sergeants in the
Kemptai didn't pick up butts. Still, he didn't want to
risk a slapping from the officer, with his damned cool
superior college-educated manner. He turned to Joshi.
He slapped him across the face and indicated the butt.
Joshi didn't hesitate. He picked it up and, walking over to
the ashtray, bearing the butt as if it was something very
precious, deposited it there. Then he bowed.

Kimura thought it was now his turn to bow and get
Tanaka's mind on to other things than his impossible
sexual desires. Let the colonel indulge in his fantasies
in his own time and not that of the Imperial Japanese
Army. He did so and drew his breath in sharply in a
token of respect, though he felt no respect at all for
Colonel Tanaka.

Tanaka took his eyes off the unconscious Eurasian
woman reluctantly. Perhaps, he told himself, if he were
alone and had more time to play with her, it might work.

But he knew that damned upstart Kimura. He was 100
per cent duty. Some said he was a secret Christian from
Nagasaki and he'd heard all those damned Christians were
like that. No time for anything. Always working, filled
with an overriding sense of duty. He sighed and put his
pistol back into the holster, noting instinctively just how

smoothly the gun's steel hardness slid into the warm, worn leather of the tight holster. '*Hai?*' he growled.

Kimura bowed once again. Tanaka wasn't impressed. He knew the elegant young man with his college airs and graces felt not one gram of respect for him, the old soldier who had served his Imperial Majesty, Hirohito, for so many years in so many foreign lands. 'Well?' he demanded.

'It is clear, sir, that the woman will not talk – not now at least. I thought if she did it would clarify things.' The young officer gave a slight shrug. Typical civilian, Tanaka told himself. A regular Japanese officer would not have dared move a muscle when speaking with a superior officer. He deserved his face to be slapped.

'So?'

'Sir, with your gracious permission, I think we ought to talk about the matter, just the two of us, if the colonel would oblige.'

Tanaka would dearly have loved to have replied, 'But the colonel will *not* oblige.' But he did not. Kimura, the clever hound, was a coming man back at HQ in Tokyo. It would be better if he humoured him. He was enjoying this sinecure in Singapore. He had no intention of going back to commanding an infantry regiment in remotest Manchuria or in some goddam remote jungle outpost in Burma. So, he said, 'As you wish, Kimura. Follow me. See the woman is looked after, Sergeant Uchida. I shall want to speak to her myself later when she has regained consciousness.'

The enlisted men clicked to attention, as Tanaka swept out, his fat buttocks trembling visibly in the riding breeches which he affected, followed by Lieutenant Kimura, who was bowing yet again.

They crossed the inner compound. It was filled with

53

prisoners, watched over by soldiers with fixed bayonets, all of them wearing cotton face masks. An emaciated beggar, half naked, rattled his tin at the colonel. Perhaps the coolie was blind or stupid, perhaps both. It was a foolish move to make at all events. Tanaka bellowed. One of the guards rushed at the coolie and smashed the brass-shod butt of his rifle into the prisoner's face. He went reeling back, his face looking as if someone had just thrown a handful of strawberry preserve at it.

Kimura frowned. All this brutality, he told himself, was counter-productive. Admittedly these prisoners were the trash of Singapore. But they were still Asiatics, the kind of people that Tokyo wanted to win over to their new Co-Prosperity Sphere. Why turn them against Japan? Apart from that, he didn't believe that brutality brought the kind of results they of Intelligence wanted. He sighed. It was hard to be a Japanese and a conqueror at the same time. There were simply too many people like Tanaka who always got things wrong. In the end they'd alienate their fellow Asiatics and one day, he knew instinctively, they would need them if they were going to retain the territory they had conquered since 1941.

Tanaka slumped heavily into his seat. He was sweating heavily again. All the same he took a bottle of Scotch from his desk drawer and a glass and poured himself a large shot. He knew it would make him sweat even more. But he needed it after the woman. He pointed to the bottle of cheap sake, the kind that the enlisted men were allowed, and grunted, 'Drink.'

Kimura bowed as if he had been given a great gift. He poured himself a very small bowlful. He didn't approve of drinking during duty hours. But Tanaka was his chief. He raised his bowl in toast.

Tanaka ignored it and gasped slightly as the powerful

spirit hit the back of his throat. Next instant he felt the surge of alcoholic warmth shoot through his gross body. For a few moments, he knew, it would renew his flagging energy, enough time at least to deal with this damned college man. 'Well, Lieutenant, where's the fire? What's all this business about, eh?' He gave his subordinate what he took to be a keen look.

Kimura didn't meet his gaze. Instead, keeping his eyes lowered, as befitted his inferior rank, he said, 'Colonel, sir, I have my doubts about what we took to be the sabotaging of our ships here last month.'

'What's that supposed to mean, Kimura?'

'With all due respect, I think we of the Kemptai were wrong in our suspicions. I don't think it was done by the locals.'

Tanaka poured himself another drink. He had signed the report back to Kemptai HQ in Tokyo that the culprits had been dealt with. His name was on the relevant documents; he was responsible for the official findings. 'Idiot!' he cursed sharply. 'What is this nonsense supposed to mean?'

'It is my contention, sir,' Kimura answered calmly, in no way offended by the insult – he had been expecting it – 'that those ships were sunk from outside Singapore.'

'*Outside!*'

'Yes, by English shipborne raiders. These commandos of which the English talk a great deal these days.'

'Impossible!' Tanaka bellowed at him. 'I authorized the execution of the saboteurs myself. It was done from here, I tell you, Kimura.'

'Yessir!' the young officer replied, his voice steady and level. He knew he'd outplay the fat pervert in the end. He wasn't going to lose his temper now and get himself fired before he was in a position to show to Tokyo just what an incompetent fool this 'friend of General Tojo' really was. 'Perhaps you'll allow me to show you this, sir?' Before Tanaka could object, he pulled the photo from its protective folder and placed it in front of his commander on the desk.

Tanaka's first impulse was to sweep it from his desk with a quick blow. Then, when he saw the outline of the naked man on the photo, he caught himself in time. One never knew with clever young buggers like Kimura. It was perhaps wiser to listen to what he had to say. So he waited.

Kimura wasted no more time. 'The picture is of a crewman from one of the ships that went down. He was picked up by one of our patrol boats some fifty miles off Singapore, Colonel. He had been wounded twice before he died.' He paused and let Tanaka absorb the information.

Tanaka stopped drinking. '*Fifty miles off Singapore . . . wounded twice*,' he echoed, hardly recognizing his own voice as he realized the full impact of the young officer's words.

'Yes, Colonel.'

'But how?'

'We hoped to get some information from the Eurasian woman – she's half Tamil and half—'

Tanaka waved him to cease talking. 'She was his whore?'

'Yes. She has heard stories.'

'Rumours?'

'Perhaps, sir. But they might explain how a crewman from the *Yarroma* came to be found way out in the ocean, when the ship was supposedly sunk by local saboteurs, Colonel.' Kimura allowed himself a careful smile. He'd got the perverted fat bastard. He was listening now all right.

Two

The sun cut their eyes like the blade of a sharp knife. Its rays rippled off the ocean in blinding little waves. Despite the breeze as the HMS *Porpoise* ploughed through the water at a steady ten knots, recharging her electric batteries, it was still bakingly hot, even under the canvas the sub's skipper had had rigged up next to the conning tower.

Still Colonel Lyn had insisted Pongo and the Druid should strip off and ensure that their bodies were tanned a deep brown. If, as he planned, they might have to pass as natives in the course of the proposed mission, he wanted them, at least, to look the part. He and Pongo were indeed wearing white breechclouts like the Japs did when they were off duty. Not the Druid. His Baptist upbringing wouldn't allow of such nakedness. So he wore long Army-issue underpants – 'drawers, cellular', as the quartermaster called them – which aroused the mirth and occasional wolf whistles from the sub's crew when they spotted them every time they were allowed on deck to escape the stiffling, stinking heat of the *Porpoise*'s interior.

They had had a long journey in the crowded mine-laying sub, packed with the top secret Sleeping Beauties, other equipment for the proposed mission and the three extra hands, themselves. Much of the way across the Bay

of Biscay, through the Med and on to the canal had been
done underwater and, for the extra hands, 'hot-bunking'*,
the lack of privacy was hard to bear. The messy routine
of using the heads and pumping their waste products out
only when the skipper gave the signal for them to do so
was another trial. For the Germans still dominated the
western Mediterranean and were always on the lookout
for English subs trying to run the narrows between Sicily
and the North African coast.

For the last few days as they headed slowly for Ceylon
and Lord Mountbatten's Supreme Headquarters, the trip
had been much easier and more relaxed; they had been
allowed to stay on the deck for long hours at a time,
getting darker and darker and discussing the new op.

But as the skipper, Commander Marsham, warned them
in that casual manner of submarine commanders, who had
to make light of their highly dangerous profession, 'Enjoy
the cakes and ale, chaps, while you can. The closer we get
to Ceylon, the more likely we're going to run into the little
yellow men. They hover around Ceylon with their planes
and destroyers like bees around honey.'

'But what are they after?' Pongo had asked. 'There's
no fighting in Ceylon. The battle's way up on the Indian
frontier with Burma.'

'Yes, agreed,' the young commander answered. His
hair was already beginning to grow grey despite the fact
that he could hardly be thirty. 'There are the convoys
taking supplies to India, and our chaps of the Fourteenth Army, and you can bet your bottom dollar that
their recce planes are keeping a watchful eye on the
goings-on at Mountbatten's HQ.' Suddenly he looked

*i.e. taking it in turns to use the crew hammocks when ratings went on
and off watch.

58

untypically solemn, as if he knew more than he was telling them.

Lyn had caught the note of disdain in the naval officer's voice and wondered what the 'goings-on' were. Still, he remained silent and listened as the submarine commander ended.

'So, gents, when you hear that bell ring –' he indicated the alarm on the conning tower above – 'run like hell! You'll have seconds before the yellow men start attacking.'

They agreed they would and then forgot the warning as, surrounded by maps of Australia and the sea routes leading to Singapore, they concentrated on the thousand and one tasks they had to undertake in preparing for Operation Malay Tiger, once Mountbatten had given his approval.

Lyn had already picked out a training area for his Sleeping Beauties and his volunteers, if he could find enough Australian and British servicemen available for volunteering. For Australia was scraping the barrel to supply troops to aid the Yanks and at the same time to defend itself in case the Japanese invaded, which still seemed likely.

'Careening Bay near Fremantle in Western Aussie. Here.' He pointed it out to Pongo and the Druid, who were going to be the nucleus of his training staff. 'It's nice and remote and the harbour's deep enough for the sub which will take us within striking distance of Singapore.'

The Druid, who was having difficulty in keeping up his knee-length drawers – pulled at the slack waistband once more and asked, 'What about using some of the lads who were with us on Operation Jaywick, sir? There must be half a dozen of 'em still left in Aussie.'

'Good question,' Pongo agreed.

Lyn frowned, and took his eyes off the map in that instant, but missed the black dot which appeared silently on the horizon to the east. 'I take your point. But I don't want to put anybody through the same kind of ordeal so soon again. It was damned nerve-racking. New blood might be better.'

Pongo grinned. 'Don't know what they're letting themselves in for, eh?'

Lyn shared his grin. The big ex-rugby player was a good soldier and an even better friend. Pongo knew only too well what *he* was letting himself in for: a bloody dangerous mission and, if he was unlucky, an unpleasant death at the end of some sadistic Jap's samurai sword. Yet he had not once attempted to back out, even back in the UK, when he could have gone back to his old unit and spent his time drinking and whoring and training for a D-Day that might well never come.

The Druid was another. Lyn laughed about the long-faced Welshman's Holy Joe manner and his prissy, old maid's attitude to drink and women – the only things that made the average fighting soldier's short brutal life bearable – as did the other ranks. All the same, he was a loyal, brave and dependable soldier. He had never once attempted to get out of what was to come, though he too could have got himself into some battalion medical team; with his experience of combat conditions, the average battalion MO would have welcomed him with open arms. Why, the Druid would have been promoted medical sergant before he had been able to sing the first verse of 'Men of Harlech'.

The two of them accepted the CO's thinking and the planning continued. On the horizon the black dot circled and then hovered there, as if suspended in the sky, wondering whether it should go on or not. On the bridge, he rating on air watch yawned. The heat and the boredom of a flat featureless ocean were getting to him. He was letting his mind wander, imagining the great foaming glasses of ice-cold beer he'd knock back once they had docked in Ceylon. There might even be women. It seemed so long since he had last had a bit in Pompey, he'd almost forgotten what to do.

The faint noise to the east as the black dot started to head west startled him out of his heat-induced reverie. He swung the huge glasses attached to a stanchion on the conning tower around. Immediately the shape of a plane ran into the clear calibrated glass of the powerful binoculars. The young rating swallowed hard. His mind ran through the recognition tables of Jap planes that he had learnt by heart. Then he had it. It was a Betty, the name the Allies had given to the Japanese long-range bomber. He didn't hesitate a second. He hit the alarm button. In the same instant that the shrill tone broke the torpid heaviness of the tropical afternoon, he yelled at the top of his voice. '*Alarm . . . Get below!*'

The soldiers needed no prompting. They had been through one drill just after they had left Portsmouth and they knew the submarine's skipper, as young as he was, tolerated no tardiness at such moments. His craft was at stake. As he had told them with unusual firmness for him, 'If you don't make the conning tower in time, gents, forget it. I'm submerging. You'd better be good swimmers after that.' Caught by surprise as they were this lazy afternoon, they reacted swiftly enough – none of them wanted to attempt to swim to Ceylon five hundred miles away.

They came skidding down the interior conning tower ladder as they had been taught, one after another, landing at the bottom in a confused heap, while above them, the lookout tightened the screws of the conning tower hatch with flying fingers. Next instant Commander Marsham was giving orders swiftly, but with no sign of panic or urgency in his voice. 'Flood tanks . . . take her down . . .'

The rest of his words were drowned by the first of the bombs from the Jap plane exploding close by. HMS *Porpoise* lurched violently. Another followed. It was even closer. Glass dials splintered. Plates sprang a leak. Rivets burst. Suddenly everything was controlled confusion.

Neither Marsham nor his crew seemed to notice as the three soldiers, shaken and nervy, retreated out of the way, as the various skilled ratings got on with their tasks, restoring the trim, checking for leaks, glueing their ears to the various bits of apparatus, checking for any surface movement as well.

'Take her down to a hundred,' Marsham commanded.

The submarine started to sink rapidly. Another bomb exploded directly overhead. The boat shook. But this time the force of the explosion was muffled somewhat by the water.

'Fifty more,' Marsham commanded again.

The Jap bombs followed the *Porpoise* as she dived deeper and deeper. Time and time again, the submarine was punched from side to side by their explosions. It was as if some gigantic fist was slamming into the 'tin can', as her crew called her. But the tin can was surprisingly tough. More glass dials splintered. Again rivets shot out of the plates. There were more and more leaks, with the off-duty men pushing their way through the crowded boat back and forth, trying to plug the rushing water before it became too much for the hard-pressed submarine.

But although Lyn knew little of the dangers of aerial attack on submarines, he could sense the bombs were not having their initial effect. They were exploding much too far above the submarine to do any more serious damage. All the same, the young skipper was taking no chance. He ordered the crew to take the *Porpoise* down another fifty. He followed that with a curt, 'Stop engines!' and a moment later, 'Silent running.'

As the bombing started to die away and the electric motors ceased their steady hum, a strange eerie silence descended upon the green-lit interior of the sub. But watching the sweat-glazed, strained faces of the crew, Lyn knew that the danger wasn't over. Every man, down to the humble cooks in the dirty whites, was listening, each wrapped in a fearful cocoon of his own thoughts; and the soldier knew what they were listening for as the bombing ceased altogether: the sound of ship engines racing their way. For the skipper obviously reckoned the Japanese wouldn't let such a prize target as a British submarine get away. They would have summoned up their surface craft to continue the attack.

Time passed with leaden feet. In the submarine, the temperature began to rise. The men's singlets were black with sweat, their strained faces as if glazed with vaseline. Acrid fumes began to seep in from the batteries. One or more of them had obviously been broken by the bombing. Quietly, as if he was just making polite chit-chat, the skipper said, 'Petty Officer, stand by with the potash masks.' He meant the masks which might be needed against the acrid poisonous fumes from the batteries if they started to get too dangerous. A moment later the crewmen were grabbing the ugly masks hurriedly, even greedily like children who felt their precious sweets might be taken away from them if they weren't quick enough. Lyn realized as the pressures on his own chest started to mount that he was gasping for breath like some ancient asthmatic in the throes of a final attack. Next to him the Druid looked at his CO, dark Celtic eyes full of worry. Lyn forced a smile. 'Don't worry,' he gasped. 'I'll survive . . . We'll all—'

He stopped short. At one of the hydrophones a leading hand had turned and had whispered solemnly to the skipper, 'Sir, ship's engines . . . approaching fast.'

They all knew what that meant. It was some sort of a Jap craft, probably a fast destroyer coming in for the attack. Next to Lyn, Pongo intoned with mock solemnity, 'For what we're about to receive, may the Good Lord make us truly thankful.'

Lyn told himself they were good chaps – Pongo and the Druid – and then he tensed for what he knew was to come.

It did.

A tremendous hammer blow at the hull. The sub quivered. Men shouted in sudden panic. Others grabbed hastily for stanchions to support themselves. A metal bowl ran the length of the deck. The *Porpoise* heeled frighteningly.

For one terrifying moment Lyn thought she might turn turtle and commence that last dive to the bottom of the ocean. But she didn't. Then the screw noises were departing rapidly as their unknown assailant raced ahead and prepared to turn for yet another attack.

Three

The urgent message went up the chain of command. It did so very rapidly for the huge Far Eastern Headquarters in Ceylon. Usually messages could get lost for hours on end, sometimes for days. There were simply far too many staff officers clinging to their nice comfortable office jobs on the island who wanted to see the messages in order to put their initials on them to prove that they actually existed and were doing some sort of job. The trick was, as they said to each other when they were in their cups, 'Keep your bowels open, your nose clean and your desk cluttered.'

But this particular signal from HMS *Porpoise* reached the Supreme Commander personally within two hours of it having been dispatched some place in the infinite waste of the Indian Ocean. More surprising even: Lord Louis Mountbatten, the Supreme Commander himself, actually deigned to read it.

Now he sat stiff and upright at his great antique desk, clad in immaculate whites, his manly chest ablaze with medal ribbons, looking every inch the handsome newly created admiral that he was. Although his eyes weren't too good, he disdained glasses – vanity was one of his many weaknesses – and he held the signal at quite some distance as he read the wording. '*Under attack enemy air and surface craft . . . In view of mission urgently request assistance Marsham.*'

With his photographic memory and almost pedantic attention to detail, Mountbatten knew who Marsham was. Indeed, if he had been asked, he might well have been able to reel off the details of the young commander's naval career; when he had entered Dartmouth, when he had been commissioned, the ships he had sailed on, even the results of his submarine commanders' course. As Mountbatten's more cynical staff officers said behind the King's cousin's back, 'Dickie probably knows if you've got soft chancre before you do and you start pissing in ten different ways.' It was a crude enough comment but typical of those who thought that, due to his connections at court, Mountbatten, the ex-destroyer captain, had been promoted well above his ability. That and his overweening vanity and ambition didn't, those who were at the sharp end of the fighting thought, make for an effective commander of all British Empire fighting forces in the whole of the Far East.

Now, however, surprisingly, Mountbatten made a very quick decision. He looked up at the expectant air and naval staff officers, waiting with their notebooks and pencils at the ready. 'Signal Cape Town, Air and Naval, plus all Royal Navy's ships in the immediate neighbourhood to go to the rescue of the *Porpoise* at once. Top priority and max effort. All right, get to it.'

Hastily the two officers scribbled down the Supreme Commander's orders and fled to the signals offices. Mountbatten, for his part, looked thoughtful for a moment – probably to impress on the other staff officers that he was giving the matter of the *Porpoise* great thought – before rising and striding to the great map of the South-East area of operations which covered the whole of the wall behind his desk.

In his new appointment as Supreme Commander, he

knew he had a hell of a job out there in that great land mass. Not only was he now commanding Indian, British, American, Chinese troops and God knows who else, he was confronted by a demoralized British Fourteenth Army. It had been badly beaten by the Japanese in 1942 and even now for every man wounded in the Fourteenth, 126 were casualties caused by sickness. That indicated to him that there was a lot of lead-swinging going on or that the junior Army commanders weren't looking after their men well enough to ensure that they didn't have such a tremendous sick rate.

But whatever the cause, Mountbatten knew he had to do something about the state of his troops' morale. He had already ensured that the footsloggers had more comforts, as they were called; but mobile breweries, which were now doing their rounds to give the soldiers the feeling that they were back at home in their local drinking a pint, weren't enough. The troops needed a victory: anything that would show them that the Japs weren't invincible.

At the beginning of the battle for Burma, most of his British soldiers had thought of the Japanese as little yellow men who wore glasses and could not shoot straight to save their lives. Now they imagined the Japs to be superhuman creatures who were just as much at home in the jungle as were the wild creatures which inhabited it.

It was for that reason he had already approved Operation Malay Tiger – the name alone was worth a battalion of infantry simply on account of its bold ring. If the as yet unknown Colonel Lyn could pull off another successful strike in Singapore, Mountbatten would ensure the news of this great victory would be spread throughout his command; and not only there. The whole world would have to know. His vanity demanded it.

He frowned abruptly, while behind him his staff officers

wondered what their chief was thinking and prepared to react at once, as Mountbatten liked them to, even to his wildest scheme; and he had plenty of those, didn't they know it.

But could this Colonel Lyn pull it off a second time? SOE Ceylon had assured him that the Japs believed the first raid had been the work of local saboteurs. But Mountbatten didn't think the Japs were bloody fools. They might well find out that it was really the work of British commandos and, if they did, would they be waiting for Colonel Lyn when he launched his second attack on Singapore? Was he, as Supreme Commander, justified in letting Operation Malay Tiger go ahead with the prospect that forty or fifty good men *and* HMS *Porpoise* might well be walking into a Jap trap?

Impatiently his staff waited, as the chief stood with his back to them staring at the huge map. What was he thinking, some of them asked themselves. Others wondered whether Lord Louis was thinking at all; or whether he was simply striking one of those dramatic poses he loved. The great warlord, alone with the problems of command, thinking out his next war-winning strategic move.

If he were, Mountbatten didn't give any indication of his thinking. Instead he turned and, in his most charming voice, said, 'I think, gentlemen, it's time for a spot of tiffin, what.'

But for all his apparent calm, Mountbatten felt uneasy that night. As always he dined under the stars with each senior officer present being attended to by his own personal servant. Everything was gleaming silver, spotless damask napkins and tablecloths, exquisite china – just like the food and wine, the best of everything. For Mountbatten didn't believe in cutting himself off from the finer things of life, even in wartime.

Yet, for all the good food, finery and attentive servants and observant junior officers who laughed uproariously at his jokes or listened earnestly to the little lectures he was fond of giving on everything from foreign decorations to the latest kind of naval telegraphy, he couldn't settle. He was not particularly worried about the *Porpoise*. If the Japs sank her, his problems would be solved right at the outset. If they didn't and Lyn and his men survived to carry out their daring mission, what then? He had just started in this new post, thanks to the King-Emperor and to a certain extent to Churchill, who already knew the great dynastic secret: Mountbatten's nephew and protégé, Prince Philip, currently a lieutenant in the Senior Service, was to be the future bridegroom of the King-Emperor's elder daughter, Elizabeth.

Now he couldn't afford a single failure. Naturally the Singapore mission was totally unimportant in the overall conduct of the war – in due course it wouldn't even make a footnote when the history of the British campaign in South-East Asia was written. But at this particular moment it was highly important to him and his reputation.

Then it came to him with the totality of a sudden vision. In essence, it didn't matter how Operation Malay Tiger turned out. If it failed it would be a glorious failure – desperate, brave young men trying to wrest back the initiative, fighting fiercely against overwhelming Japanese odds. If it succeeded it would show light at the end of the tunnel. As Winston had said recently after the Battle of El Alamein, 'It is not the beginning of the end, but perhaps the end of the beginning.'

Abruptly Mountbatten felt very pleased with himself. He beamed at the assembled staff officers, his face even more handsome in the soft light of the candles. 'Gentlemen,' he announced, 'I suddenly feel the urge to drink

69

a glass of bubbly. I wonder if you care to drink one with me?'

His offer was accepted immediately. The sycophants and the promotion-seekers didn't need to be asked twice. There were murmurs of pleasure and delighted voices exclaimed, 'Damn nice of you, sir . . . Be very glad to . . . I say, what a treat!' and the like.

The Ceylonese waiters and stewards appeared with the bottles of French champagne almost immediately. Glasses were poured, dribbles were wiped away with elegant crisp napkins, while Mountbatten waited with a winning smile on his long handsome aristocratic face. Finally he raised his flute. 'Gentlemen, I give you a toast. To Operation Malay Tiger!'

Obediently the staff officers raised their glasses, the fine crystal sparkling in the yellow light cast by the candles. They didn't know what they were toasting. It didn't matter. They were getting free bubbly. 'To Operation Malay Tiger!' they intoned as one in a deep solemn bass and then, throwing back their heads, downed the precious yellow liquid in one long greedy swallow.

The storm broke with surprising suddenness. The gentle wind abruptly became very warm and cloying. With an almighty crack, the thunder rolled across the night sky. Lightning stabbed the darkness a jagged scarlet. In an instant the wind rose to a howling crescendo. The skies opened. The rain poured down in an angry hissing solid sheet of grey. The palms bent almost double.

In a flash, all was chaos. The wind whipped the champagne glasses off the table. Menus flew back and forth. Servants, their immaculate white uniforms already soaked black, pelted after them.

'Let's run for it, chaps!' Mountbatten bellowed above

the howl of the wind and the angry hiss of the tropical rain.

Together with the soaked Supreme Commander, the
staff officers, some of them cursing the storm, others
laughing uproariously, as if they had drunk more than
a single toast to the coming operation, ran through the
pelting raindrops for the shelter of the great headquarters.

Behind them, the sweeper emerged from the bushes.
He was naked save for a pair of soaked cheap cotton
drawers. Now his brown body glistened in the rain. Not
that the sudden tropical storm seemed to worry him. He
looked like one of those downtrodden low-caste creatures
who was so used to life's adversities that nothing could
move him now save impending death. Wearily he began
to pick up the champagne glasses from the grass where
they had fallen. Most of them were broken. But that was
not his concern. Broken or whole, he placed the glasses
on the big table from which the Supreme Commander
and his staff had just fled. Each time he bent and raised
himself, leaning heavily on the broomstick to do so, he
gave a grunt, as if it were all too much for him.

Anyone watching the lone sweeper – the rest of the
servants had fled for shelter too, till the downpour abated
somewhat – would have taken him for what he was, a
broken-down, half-starved, low-caste native, trying to
support himself and probably a household of diseased
skinny kids – the wogs always had far too many kids,
it was their only pleasure – till Nature granted him the
favour of sudden death – if he was lucky. But no one
was watching the sweeper. Why should they? He was
harmless: the lowest of the lowest. He was just another
wog shitehouse wallah who deserved to remain unseen.

One by one he cleared up the glasses. Despite the rain
coming down in sheets, he paused now, leaning on his

71

broom, breathing hard as if it had been all too much for his skinny-ribbed frame. He looked at the open champagne bottles. They did not interest him. He wouldn't touch their contents anyway; his religion wouldn't allow him to do so. Perhaps he was wondering, in that slow dull manner of his kind, whether he should do something about removing them or not. Finally, it seemed, he decided that he should. One by one he started to place them next to the glasses. Once he paused and for some reason, it appeared, tried to penetrate the grey hissing gloom of the rainstorm. To no avail. Suddenly his skinny brown claws moved with remarkable speed for such a bent, worn figure. There was the gleam of metal. The sweeper shoved something down the front of his cotton drawers. His hands moved like magic. It was all done and over with in a matter of thirty seconds. Then, moving at the same slow pace as before, the sweeper, the brush carried over his bent naked shoulders, disappeared back into the bushes . . .

Four

They had been submerged over eight hours now. At first, after the initial couple of surface attacks by what appeared to be Japanese destroyers, the men of HMS *Porpoise* consoled themselves that the Nips would give up after a while. They were way off their own bases and by now the Supreme Commander's HQ would have received their request for help. Surely surface and air would be reacting by now and that meant that Japanese radar should be picking up the enemy craft on their way to do battle with them.

Nothing of that sort had taken place however. They were still at a depth of some 150 feet, being buffeted by pattern after pattern of Japanese depth charges, as their ships hurried back and forth on the surface. Now they were suffering. A lot. Breathing was becoming increasingly difficult, even though the skipper had allowed them to put on their masks at five-minute intervals. Suffocation was on the cards. Men were already beginning to rip off their sweat-soaked singlets, as if that would allow them to gain more air. But there was none.

Thirty minutes later, little had changed, save that conditions within the trapped submarine were reaching the critical stage. Now some of the younger ratings had ceased gasping for air. Their lips turned blue; they were too weak to fight for each new breath. Indeed, some of them were already, so it appeared, asleep. The old hands, the three-stripers and petty officers, just knew better. They were already in the first stage before death. Summoning up the last of their strength, they passed from rating to rating, shaking them awake, threatening those weakly ones who attempted to doze off again once they had wakened.

Lyn looked at Pongo and the Druid. They were fighting back, taking tiny breaths from the emergency mask, just sufficient to revive them and stop the noxious gases from overcoming them altogether; then carefully breathing in the fumes once again. He flashed a glance at the captain. He was setting the best example he could, refusing to use the mask, smiling weakly every time one of the crew looked in his direction pleadingly; and Lyn knew why. The dying ratings wanted a decision. It was a simple one – If we are to die, let us die on the surface in the clean fresh air, while we've still got some fight left in us.

Of course, the skipper of HMS *Porpoise* knew he had to put an end to this terrible purgatory, cost what it may. Some of the younger men wouldn't last much longer. All the same, he was a veteran. He was not going to sacrifice them and his boat to the Japs just like that. Besides, he knew if they surfaced and were taken by the Japs, they wouldn't survive long. Savage and remorseless as they were habitually, the crew would get no mercy from the enemy. Either the Japs would leave them to drown in the middle of the ocean or they'd slaughter them as they swam in the water. There would be no hope of quarter.

For hours he had been praying that he'd receive some assistance from the South African Air Force at least. He knew how long it took signals to get through, even ones of distress. But this one marked urgent shouldn't have done. All he could guess was that there was bad flying weather somewhere or other off the coast which was causing the delay. At the same time he had been hoping fervently that the Japanese would break off their attack. They hadn't. Now he knew the time had come for action. 'Piss or get off the pot,' as he whispered to himself. All the same, he wasn't just going to surface like that and allow the Japs to tamely shoot his craft to pieces. He had to have a plan.

He made his decision. He turned to his second in command. 'Number One,' he said in the firmest voice he could manage, 'tell the men to put on their potash masks and *keep* them on.'

The young lieutenant didn't argue. He guessed what the skipper was about. He wanted the men as fit as he could get them for impending action. He gave the order. Greedily the men slipped on the ugly masks and started taking great gasps of purified air.

The skipper turned to the chief petty officer. 'Take her up to periscope height, Chiefie.'

The electric motors clicked into action. Slowly the sub started to rise as the engine-room artificers adjusted the trim, knowing that they had to move swiftly despite their weakness and nausea; the Jap detectors would already be locking on to the sound of the motors.

Up the *Porpoise* went. Tension fought fatigue inside the submarine. Pongo gave Lyn the thumbs-up sign. The Druid smiled wanly and looked as if he might start praying aloud in his Welsh sing-song at any moment. New life enthused the crew. They moved back to their duty stations without orders. All of them knew, even the sickest, that their fate was going to be decided in a few minutes.

They reached the required height. At the hydrophones the masked operators tensed. They knew the Japs would have spotted them by now. Soon they'd be coming in for the attack.

'Up periscope!' the skipper commanded. There was the hiss of compressed air. Smartly the glistening metal tube rose. The skipper turned his battered white cap back-to-front, so that the peak was at the back. At any other time he would have looked slightly foolish. Not now. The situation was too serious. The crew tensed. They were like seriously ill patients waiting for some great doctor's final diagnosis.

Hurriedly the skipper adjusted the periscope. He turned up the intensifier to get a better view. Then he had her. An ugly-looking destroyer, her superstructure unmistakeably Japanese, surged towards him, a white bone in her teeth. Hurriedly he ordered, 'Periscope down.' The order was followed by 'Both ahead . . . Full.'

Suddenly the *Porpoise* trembled. She burst into full power. Immediately the ruptured plates started to leak once more. The caulking crews snapped out of their frozen poses. They started to caulk the gaps at once. The skipper turned to Lyn. 'It's going to be bloody risky . . . But it might work.'

'What?' Lyn cried above the tap-tap of the caulking hammers and the ping-ping coming from outside the hull, as the sonar bounced off the submarine, indicating that their unseen enemies above the water had already located them.

'I'm going to shelter beneath her hull this run, Colonel, if I can. If she doesn't sink us first, as soon as she turns, I'm going to slip a tin fish right up her arse . . . Stand by, Number One and Two . . . torpedoes!'

The torpedo mates needed no urging. They knew what was at stake. Swiftly the burly petty officers took up their positions next to the deadly 'tin fish' up at the bow. Each carried a ton of high explosive. It was enough to blow even the biggest Jap destroyer from here to kingdom come – that Lyn knew. The question was: could the *Porpoise* survive long enough for the captain to fire those tin fish of his?

Now all was controlled tension. The crewmen even seemed to have forgotten the lack of oxygen which had had them on their knees, dying, it seemed, only minutes before. Adrenalin surged through their blood. Their eyes gleamed above their masks. It was as if the desire for revenge had swept away all their physical disabilities. At the periscope the skipper kept glancing at the green-glowing dial of his wristwatch all the while, as if he had an important date that he wouldn't dare fail to meet. And in a way, Lyn told himself, he had. It was a date with death!

The noise was rising maddeningly. Above them they could hear the whirr of the Japanese ship's screws as it churned the water into a white fury. At the same time that ping-ping, as the sonar beam bounced off the *Porpoise*'s hull, became ever louder. It wasn't the noise level in itself that was so bad, Lyn told himself. It was instead the knowledge that the noise gave the men trapped below that they were hunted fugitives, whose lives were perhaps forfeit in a matter of minutes.

Now everything depended upon the skipper's tactics and whether he could outwit the Jap, as the *Porpoise*'s crew fought hard to get every last bit of speed out of the big submarine and keep pace with the Japanese craft, only feet above their heads. For now they could feel the backwash of the other ship, as its wake buffeted the *Porpoise*.

At the bridge, the young submarine commander tried to keep his nerve, and not reveal to the crew that he, too, was about at the end of his tether. But he could not stop the tic that had started up at the right side of his face, nor the fact that, although he constantly wiped his sweaty palms on the back of his tunic, they started to perspire again almost immediately. For he knew he was losing the race. The *Porpoise* was beginning to slip behind her unseen enemy. Once that happened the Jap would immediately begin to drop a pattern of depth charges, and with the *Porpoise* located exactly by her sonar and at this range, she couldn't miss. '*Turn . . . Oh, bloody well turn!*' a panic-stricken voice screeched at the back of his mind. But the Jap refused stubbornly to do as that voice from the depths of his brain demanded.

'Sir,' the petty officer at the hydrophone called urgently, slipping off part of his earphones, face streaming with sweat. 'She's slowing down . . . *Sir, she's turning!*'

The skipper didn't hesitate. 'Up periscope,' he commanded in a broken hoarse voice that he hardly recognized.

The tube shot upwards. He flung himself behind it. With hands that trembled wildly, he swung the periscope round. The waves heaved and swayed in front of the circle of gleaming glass. 'Hurry . . . for God's sake!' he cursed to himself. Then there she was. The Japanese destroyer swinging round in a burst of bubbling cream-white water. She was turning all right.

He hesitated no longer. He flung a look at his second in command. His number one reacted immediately. He looked up from his range table, glowing an eerie green in the dim light of the interior and rapped out range and speed without being asked. The skipper could have kissed him. That was the kind of trained subordinate that he liked. He didn't wait another second. '*Fire one!*' he yelled.

There was the hiss of rushing compressed air. The

submarine shuddered. The Druid said afterwards, the boat actually leapt in the water, but no one believed him. '*Fire two!*' Again the *Porpoise* shuddered.

Number One held up his stopwatch so that the crew, new hope dawning in their red-rimmed eyes, could see he was beginning to count off the seconds the torpedo run took. Lyn, as anxious as the rest, moved his own parched cracked lips under the mask in time with him. 'One . . . two . . . th—'

There was a muted crash. The *Porpoise* shook violently this time. At the periscope the sweating skipper yelled, 'A hit!'

Another crash. For a moment the submarine seemed to stop in the water, as if she had suddenly run into a brick wall. '*Another hit!*' the skipper cried with almost boyish enthusiasm. 'She's sinking . . . We're going up.'

As one, the crew started ripping off their masks. A burly old petty officer, red-faced and thick-nosed, who looked as if he might well have served with Nelson on the *Victory*, cried, 'Three cheers for the good old *Porpoise* . . . and the skipper. He's saved our bacon again!'

Lyn smiled as the men cheered the skipper, who turned from the periscope momentarily to face them and was now actually blushing.

Five minutes later they were on the surface, the conning tower hatch opened, letting in streams of blessed fresh air and with the gun crew running along the dripping, gleaming deck, hurrying to man the forward gun just in case.

But there was no need for that. As Lyn came on deck, followed by Pongo and the Druid, the destroyer, her back broken, was sinking rapidly. Here and there desperate Japanese sailors were jumping from the superstructure. Others, naked save for a loincloth, a kind of white bandage with red characters around their heads, were preparing to disembowel themselves. Perhaps it was the best way out for them. For the British sailors would not attempt to rescue the hated Japs. They would drown or be bait for the sharks which would be on their way to the scene soon. Druid told himself, as the first sailor plunged a knife into his belly and started to cut upwards in a sudden spurt of bright red blood, that it was wrong to commit suicide; indeed, it was a sin. But he realized he'd have to keep the knowledge to himself. The others would rag him unmercifully if he didn't do so.

Lyn watched the terrible scene in brooding silence. Generally he had little feeling for the enemy. The behaviour of the Japanese ever since they had commenced their march of conquest had been too terrible to feel sympathy for them. Yet he was moved somehow; he didn't know why. But what he did know was that he felt abruptly drained.

It was as if someone had opened an invisible tap and let all the spirit and drive drip out of his body. He watched mesmerized as a Jap sailor flung himself off the mast of the sinking ship like a high diver at a competition performing before an admiring crowd. But he failed to judge the distance correctly. Instead of plunging into the sea, he slammed into the deck. Even at that distance he thought he heard the crunch of the man's bones being smashed, though he knew it wasn't possible. Still, Colonel Lyn could not suppress a moan. Hastily he turned his head away, as if he could look no more. He had seen enough horrors for this day.

Thus it was that his batman found him. Any sound the Welshman might have made, as he approached, paused and then continued, was drowned by the last shrieks and screams of the Jap sailors already in the water. For now the sharks had scented blood and were zig-zagging in, eager for the kill. The Druid stopped when he was almost parallel with his CO. Softly, in that sing-song of his, he asked, 'Everything all right, sir?'

It seemed to take Lyn a long time to react and the Druid was just about to repeat his anxious enquiry when Lyn answered softly, 'Yes, everything's all right.' But there was no conviction in the big colonel's voice and it was then that the Welshman knew – perhaps part of that Celtic foresight attributed to his race – that Operation Malay Tiger was going to go wrong.

Book Three

The Sleeping Beauties Awake

One

'*Gentlemen, please give your attention – Now!*' The harsh metallic voice over the public address system drowned the sharp hiss and slither of the high Australian surf. On the beach the seagulls, which had been picking up the scraps dropped by the high-ranking visitors to this remote place, rose into the sky, crying plaintively like lost children. '*Raise your glasses please, gentlemen,*' the disembodied voice of the observer urged the bunch of staff officers huddled around the Supremo. '*They're coming in at three o'clock.*' There was a metallic grating, which the officers took for a laugh. '*That's to the right, for the gentlemen of the Navy.*'

Mountbatten, crisp in khaki but wearing his immaculate white Royal Navy cap, heavy with the gold leaf of a full admiral, smiled and raised his binoculars obediently. As one, his staff, who had been waiting, it seemed, for this cue, did the same.

'*Focus on the smokescreen, gentlemen . . . please,*' the speaker urged. '*They should be coming through it in a second . . .*'

Standing to one side of the top brass, Lyn didn't raise his glasses. He knew what was to come and his eyesight was so keen he could see without binoculars. Instead he kept his gaze on the second hand of his big Army-issue watch. His men were halfway through their training now and they were up to the standard that he demanded, but Lord Louis had insisted on this demonstration for some visiting Americans from MacArthur's* staff. As always, Lyn supposed, the Supremo wanted to show off. He sighed and told himself that over the years this sort of thing had become more of a public-relations exercise and less of a training scheme. Now that there was a chance of victory in the Far East, there were a lot of high-ranking people like Mountbatten who wanted to make themselves out to be the father of those victories.

Then he forgot the bullshit merchants, as he called them, and concentrated on his men's attack.

As the smokescreen started to drift away with the wind, he could just see the low sleek outline of HMS *Porpoise*, still bearing the shining steel scars of the Japanese depth-charge attack. He imagined he could also just make out the white-painted miniature destroyer painted on her conning tower, which the proud crew had daubed on in Sydney to indicate their first kill.

But his gaze was really fixed on two Sleeping Beauties that had now been dropped over the side of the big minelaying sub. They had caught the attention of the speaker, too. For he boomed through the tannoy system, *'Gentlemen, what you are seeing now is the first public demonstration of the Royal Navy's latest secret weapon – the Sleeping Beauty. Though I can assure you – as you will soon see for yourselves – those craft at the bows of the* Porpoise *are anything but sleepy.'*

There was a burst of good-humoured laughter from the top brass. Lyn wasn't surprised at their laughter. He had seen they had been well supplied with 'pusser's grog' before they had driven down to this sealed-off

---

*Gen. D. MacArthur, head of all American forces in the Pacific.

beach. The admirals and generals should be in a good mood.

Now Lyn watched as Pongo, half of the first team, sprang, remarkably lightly for his bulk, into the new craft, steadied it and, as it rose on the waves, slapping against the hull of the *Porpoise*, waited till 'Horse-arse' – the new Australian recruit, who did look a bit like a horse's rear end – prepared to follow. Lyn prayed he wouldn't fall into the water. The big lanky Australian from the outback was somewhat clumsy. He didn't. He'd taken in his training. He jumped almost cat-like and hit the canoe, his knees flexed to reduce any shock.

Next moment the second team, consisting of Blue – another Aussie but an old hand, veteran of the first operation against Singapore – and Corporal Jenkins – he was too stiff and by-the-book for a nickname – followed. Again they were successful. On the wooden tower at the head of the beach, the observer commented, '*The first obstacle has been overcome, gentlemen. Getting into the Sleeping Beauty is not as easy as it looks. She doesn't take to strangers interfering with her, ha, ha!*'

Again the top brass laughed at the weak joke. Not Lyn. He knew that Pongo and Blue would get their mates into the canoes. Now it was a question of how the Sleeping Beauties' electric motors would perform. For the swell near the gleaming white beach, flanked by palms and mangroves, was pretty heavy. It would be tricky. Hardly aware that he was doing it, he crossed the fingers of his right hand behind his back for good luck. Now came the proof of the pudding: the seaworthiness of the new craft in tropical waters and the state of training of their crews.

Hastily Pongo and Blue got into position. Gripping

the joysticks, they started to flood the ballast tanks of their craft, while the observer explained the technical details. Now the two pilots prepared to start their engines.

Lyn's crossed fingers tightened. The Sleeping Beauties were great craft. They took a great deal of the physical effort out of the task; with the motors they could arrive on the beach relatively fresh and not exhausted from all that paddling from the transporting sub. But they were temperamental and nothing more so than the electric motors. Sometimes they could be the very bitches to get started and today he wanted to get everything over and done with – then he would be able to get the brass out of his hair, what he had left of it after all these years of living off nerves.

Pongo's motor started. He nosed the secret craft into the waves, lowering the Sleeping Beauty so that it presented hardly any silhouette at all. In an emergency the Sleeping Beauty could penetrate the sea to a depth of seven metres. But Lyn wasn't going to try that particularly tricky manoeuvre in the presence of the big shot and in the tricky offshore swell. Blue's motor followed. He nosed his way closer to the leading craft.

On his tower, the man commenting rather like a tennis umpire stayed silent. He'd been ordered by Lyn to keep the chat to a minimum once the craft were launched. He shouldn't promise anything to the brass and then be shown he couldn't keep the promises when – and if – something went haywire.

But the top brass's attention was fixed exclusively on the twin boats. They didn't need a commentary. They could see how the two boats were a remarkable change from the traditional folboats used by commandos. They were gliding through the sea noiselessly, barely visible, not even a flurry of white that someone steering with a paddle in the conventional manner might display.

Time passed. The group of big shots were entranced. Lyn could see Mountbatten, keeping his gaze fixed on the Sleeping Beauties, was at the same time dictating notes to his military secretary; and the commando colonel had the feeling that they were positive and complimentary. He hoped so, at least.

Now the craft were approaching the supposed entrance to the harbour, just as they would do soon at Singapore – God willing. Pongo, slightly in the lead, cut his engine speed. Although Lyn could not see the manoeuvre, he knew what his second in command was doing. He was easing back the joystick. Then briefly he would open the Sleeping Beauty's ballast tanks. This Pongo would control with his thumbs, keeping down the rate at which the compressed air was allowed to enter the ballast tanks. By doing this he would avoid any sudden bubbling of the water which might well give away his position to any watching enemy.

It was a tricky business, Lyn knew. But with practice any Sleeping Beauty pilot would be able to do it so neatly that not even a gull balancing on the waves nearby would be disturbed and rise in flight, again possibly giving the craft's position away. Why, a good pilot could even 'porpoise', as they called the manoeuvre, which brought the craft out of the water for a fleeting moment so that he could get a brief glimpse of his surroundings and get his bearings.

But Lyn need not have worried about Pongo. He had absorbed his hard training expertly and now he was moving on, the manoeuvre completed. Lyn signalled to the commentator that now the tactic had been a success, he could inform the puzzled top brass what they had just seen. He did so now while Lyn raised his glasses and watched Blue and Corporal Jenkins prepare to go through the same manoeuvre.

But it wasn't the second Sleeping Beauty which caused the trouble subsequently. It was the first, Pongo's and Horse-arse's. Now they were heading straight into the surf. It was high. But Pongo was confident that he could manage it; he had sailed through worse in an ordinary folboat, powered solely by paddles. Apparently Horse-arse didn't share the officer's confidence. For through his glasses Lyn could see the alarm crossing the Australian's extraordinarily ugly face. Next moment he seemed to want to rise from the Sleeping Beauty. It was a fatal move to make.

In a flash everything went wrong. Desperately Pongo tried to keep the boat upright. To no avail! She overturned and next instant the two of them, the captain and the new Australian recruit, were in the fierce tidal race, arms splashing and slapping the water furiously as they tried to keep from going under. Lyn, the exercise totally forgotten, was shrilling crazily on his service whistle for the rescue team to get them out of the sea before it was too late . . .

Mountbatten didn't pull his punches. That charming good-natured smile of his was gone. Instead it had been replaced by an angry blazing-eyed look that must have frightened many a poor teenaged rating when he had been a destroyer flotilla captain at the beginning of the war.*
'It's not good enough, Lyn,' he snapped, as, outside, the brass, well plied with more spirits, Scotch this time, filed to the waiting staff cars, where the gold-braided lackeys, with their great glittering lanyards, bowed and scraped and

*See D. Harding, *Sink the Kelly*, for further details.

got them into the Packards and Humbers. 'We can't have slip-ups like that at this stage of the game, you know. In one fell swoop you lost half your attack force and if there had been an enemy out there, he would have soon heard and dealt with the remaining half. Is that clear?'

'Yessir,' Lyn answered unhappily. It was no use trying to defend himself or his men, although they had had such a short time to prepare for this exercise. He knew Mountbatten wouldn't listen anyway. He didn't want excuses; he wanted results and that was that. 'I'll take care of it, sir.'

'See that you do,' Mountbatten said icily and barely answered Lyn's salute. With that he was gone to his own splendid staff car, flying the Supreme Commander's pennant.

The Druid looked sadly at his CO as Mountbatten departed. Not Pongo. Indignantly he snorted, 'Pompous arsehole! What did he expect after three weeks of training?'

'The best, Pongo.'

'But look at the material we've been able to find. Aussie's scraped clean of good chaps. All we've got, except for a few old hands, is Horse-arse.' He frowned. 'He's not exactly Brains' Trust material, is he?' He referred to the BBC's popular radio show, featuring intellectuals who seemed to be able to answer any and every question levelled at them.

'Ner, he ain't.' A voice broke into their conversation as they stood there waiting for the top brass to depart. 'He's a frigging thick, grog-guzzling abo, that's what he is!'

Lyn swung round and stared at his mixed bunch of Britishers and Australians. 'Who said that?' he demanded.

But no one replied, not even Horse-arse, whose phenomenally ugly face had flushed red. Suddenly Colonel

91

Lyn realized that he had another kind of trouble on his hands. He knew his Aussies. If Horse-arse really was an aborigine, an 'abo', sooner or later there'd be a showdown – and a showdown was the last thing that Operation Malay Tiger needed at the moment.

Two

From the main railway terminus at Sydney's Circular Quay, the local ferries carried passengers across the harbour to the North Shore suburbs. The furthest of these was the holiday area of Manly. The ferry to Manly carried not only civilian passengers, but also the mostly middle-aged or very young garrison troops who were stationed on the North Headland and the ocean beaches which ran for miles along the coast.

'Now chaps,' Lyn said, after he believed his men had had time to read the simple blurb he had prepared for them to explain the basic outline of the exercise. 'That main Manly ferry route passes over the anti-submarine boom. Everyone at the top believes that the boom is impregnable and the boom ships' crews have become slack. They're on to a cushy number, they think, and all they live for is their fag ration and a chance at the local ladies of the night.' He waited for the expected cries of delight, naughty suggestions and the demands for an immediate transfer to the boom ships – and he got them.

Lyn smiled. In the last three weeks since Mountbatten had torn a strip off him for the failure of the second Sleeping Beauty, he had worked his men from dawn to dusk remorselessly. Despite that, or perhaps because of it, his fifty-odd old hands and new recruits seemed in fine fettle. They actually seemed to be looking forward to the tough, perhaps even dangerous, training exercise that he had planned for them now.

'Naturally the Royal Australian Navy –' he raised his hand to stop the jeers and the expected raspberries – 'know all about subs. They know their tricks and believe anyway the Japs wouldn't dare tackle a target like Sydney. Why, the authorities haven't even ordered a blackout for the city.' He lowered his voice momentarily to gain their full attention. 'But it's not Jap subs that are going to attack, it's our Sleeping Beauties, and I can say this with confidence now.' He raised his voice for the punchline he had thought out already. 'They're in for the bloody biggest surprise they've ever had!'

The men, especially the Aussies among them, whistled with delight and stamped their heavy ammunition boots on the floor, although it was their own fellow Australians who were in for 'the bloody biggest surprise they've ever had'.

'Now then, chaps.' Lyn silenced them with his raised hands. 'It's not going to be easy, although this is only a training exercise to show the powers-that-be what we can do. We're going to go in from a position about thirty-odd miles from Sydney's North Head.'

His audience looked impressed. That was a long way out and the Australians among them knew that; in addition, there was always a choppy, even rough sea in that area. It was going to be a hard slog. Still no one raised an objection.

'We'll sail into Sydney harbour and attach our dummy limpets to any ship that we can. Now I know this is only a training exercise, but I want us to take it deadly serious. We want to prove that we can do as I've just said.' He smiled at them confidently. 'In particular, to you know who – and no rude comments, *please*.'

Again his audience was amused and Lyn knew he had them. They knew the dangers. Nature, after all, didn't take sides. The good chaps were just as likely to be killed by the sea, the wind and the tide as the bad 'uns. But Lyn wasn't going to allow them the time to brood about the possible dangers of the exercise. As a good commander he knew he had to give his men something pleasant to look forward to after the exercise. So, he ended with, 'Once it's over, chaps, Sydney is yours for twenty-four hours.'

That did it. The men couldn't be restrained, especially the Australians. After nearly six weeks of hard training on that remote coast, without a woman or a pub within a hundred miles, the thought of both in a few hours' time set them off whistling and cheering crazily, leaving Lyn to get down from the box from which he had addressed them and turn to a grinning Pongo. 'It's going to be a hot time in the old town tonight, Pongo. The Aussie redcaps are going to have their work cut out for them, I think.'

'You can say that again, sir,' Pongo agreed and then, lowering his voice, he added, 'I can't say I'd object to getting the heavy water off my own manly chest, Ivan.' He winked.

Lyn's grin broadened. 'You deserve it, old chap. But remember, don't come back with a souvenir of Sydney's red-light district. Now, let's get one last look at the set-up while we wait for the Met people's forecast.' He threw a glance at the sky over the sea. It was darkening, for it was getting closer to dusk. At the same time, he noticed the wind was rising, which didn't seem too promising for the vital exercise which he'd planned to convince Mountbatten that his men were now as fully trained as they ever were going to be. If he carried on the day-after-day routine out in the wilderness, the men would grow stale.

95

'All right.' He bent over the charts of Sydney Bay again. 'One last time, Pongo . . .'

They cast off from the *Porpoise* at two in the morning. As Lyn had guessed, the weather was not good. The wind was coming in from the west in moderate force. All the same, the sea was rough with a fair swell running, which had made it difficult for the men to clamber into their Sleeping Beauties. But they'd managed it without a single casualty; and the bad weather did have the advantage of giving them the cover they needed if they were going to penetrate the crowded habour without being detected.

Thereafter they made good progress despite the swell and soon they were beginning to spot the lights of Outer and Inner South Head. Further on they could also just catch glimpses of brightness and, at the graving dock on the Garden Island, they could see the floodlights. Obviously a night shift was doing some urgent repairs to shipping probably damaged by Jap submarines, which were everywhere in the Indian Ocean these days.

Lyn, in the lead together with Druid as his number two, told himself that one day soon, he hoped, it would be the turn of the Japs to take casualties; they'd run the show in the Far East too bloody long. Then he concentrated on his navigation, knowing that the rest of his Sleeping Beauty crews were zeroing on him.

Travelling at the maximum four and a half knots, ignoring the rise and fall of the flimsy small craft which could make the most experienced of old seadogs spill his guts, they approached the new anti-torpedo boom which was being constructed between George's Head on Middle Head and Green Point on Inner South Head. When he had first spotted the obstruction during his initial recce dressed in rough docker's clothing, Colonel Lyn's heart had sunk. He had told himself it was going to be damnably tough for his Sleeping Beauties to get through the thick steel wire mesh. Then he had spotted the fact that the workmen and engineers had not been too thorough. For some reason known only to themselves they had left small gaps at both ends of the anti-torpedo boom. They weren't big. But they were big enough for his craft to slip through in single file, which was now his intention. There was only one catch. The Sydney Harbour Foreshore Authority employed a large number of civilians in their Maritime Service Board. It was their job to patrol on land – and on sea in small boats – and report anything suspicious to naval headquarters by short-wave radio.

Lyn reasoned, as he lowered speed and headed for the gap, the Sleeping Beauty very deep in the water now and making hardly a ripple on the surface, that if one of the civvy watchmen spotted them, all hell would be let loose. There might even be casualties. For, although the senior officers at Naval HQ had been warned of the penetration exercise, for security reasons, shipmasters and the like hadn't. If the alarm were given, there'd be a good chance that some trigger-happy ship's gunner would start attempting to blow them out of the water. He sighed. But that was a chance they'd have to take. He concentrated on the task ahead of him.

He reduced speed even more. Now they were creeping into the gap, with the nearest sea wall perhaps a hundred yards away. Behind him, the Druid, muffled in his frogsuit, peered to left and right, trying to spot the first sign of danger. Lyn felt his nerves begin to tingle electrically, too. This was only an exercise, he knew – all the same it *could* end in casualties if he made a balls-up of things.

The minutes passed. Unknown to Colonel Lyn, he was traversing a stretch of water which had gone down in

Australian history, for in May 1770, Captain Cook had sailed his *Discovery* through the very same waters. But in the summer of 1943 Colonel Lyn neither knew nor cared about the historic exploits of his fellow Yorkshireman. For he had just caught the first sounds of a slow-moving light craft coming in the direction of the gap, too.

He reacted immediately. In a flash he had turned off the electric motor and grabbed a paddle. The Druid didn't need to be ordered to do the same. He took up his own paddle, poised low in the Sleeping Beauty and waited for instructions as Lyn strained and peered through the purple darkness of the tropical night.

Then he saw it. It was what he took to be a Maritime Service skiff, which would mean it would be manned by watchmen, who were paid to look out for suspicious craft and objects. The men on the deck of the skiff weren't the ordinary bored sleepy watch, one found on merchant ships. These were trained – and armed – observers. If anything went wrong now, it could mean a disastrous and rapid end to the planned Operation Malay Tiger.

Behind him the rest of the Sleeping Beauties, spread out in single file, switched off and paddled deeper into the shadows, carefully letting the air out of their buoyancy tanks so that the craft sank lower and lower. Now they waited and those who believed in God suddenly started praying. Indeed, the Druid was reciting a whole service in his brain, including a miners' choir singing in Welsh. Fortunately it all took place in his head and in total silence.

The skiff came closer. Lyn was in a quandary. Should he chance it and hope it would pass without spotting him? Or should he declare his presence now and obviate a possible outbreak of firing? He still had time to do so. But if he did, he knew he'd risk the whole mission. His face contorted with misery as he pondered the options, while the skiff came closer and closer.

Suddenly – startlingly – luck and chance took a hand. The first flares exploded in the sky above Sydney. In a burst of brilliant light they hung in the heavens, casting around them a cold silver hue. For a moment it seemed the whole of the great Australian city was too startled to do anything.

Then everything happened at once. The air-raid sirens began to shrill their dire warning. To the east there came the first menacing drum roll of anti-aircraft fire. Tracer zipped lethally upwards in the same instant that the Japanese bombers commenced releasing their deadly load.

Later Lyn would swear that he distinctly heard someone on the deck of the skiff swear, 'Fuck this for a game o' soldiers,' followed by the engine of the little craft picking up immediately as her skipper decided that it would be wiser to get out of the harbour while he still had time. For it was obvious that it was the shipping tightly packed into the great anchorage that the Japs were after.

Lyn for his part didn't waste a second. Hastily he restarted the engines, telling himself that what he and his men were going to do now was absolutely crazy. They were about to place dummy bombs on the first ships they could reach, while above them somewhere, the Japanese bomber pilots were attempting to sink those selfsame ships with real ones. 'Totally absolutely crackers!' he roared aloud, the pressure off, while all around his secret little fleet, the water heaved and spurted as bomb after bomb exploded . . .

Three

The morning was bright with warm sunshine. Even the bomb-shattered buildings along the shoreline didn't look too bad in the sun's rays. They had taken on a mellow look so that the crowds of civilians and servicemen, mostly Americans, walking the streets gazed at the damaged places as if they were some great tourist attraction.

The men of Colonel Lyn's commando, tired but triumphant, were naturally not one bit interested in the bomb ruins, tourist attraction or not. After the severe regime of their remote training base, they were concerned solely with the two things that lightened the hard lot of the average soldier – beer and bints. As they pushed their way through the slow-moving throng on the seafront, they wise-cracked using the ancient, traditional joke of leavemen throughout the ages: 'Anybody knows the second thing a squaddie does when he comes home to his missus – *he takes his pack off!*' Hoary old joke that it was, it caused great outbursts of happy laughter.

Naturally, this being Australia, the bars were not yet open – *officially*. But the Aussies among the commando knew where they'd find a drink even at this time of the morning. 'And a bit o' the other, cobber, as well,' as they assured their English mates confidently. 'That is,' as Blue intoned with a significant look at Horse-arse, 'if yer a white man. Too many ruddy blacks here as it is, with all them bleeding black nigger Yanks.'

Horse-arse clenched his big fists, but the Druid restrained him quickly with a whispered, 'Let us go and find the Sally Ann, something like that. Get us a nice cup o' char, mate.'

For a moment, Horse-arse looked as if he might refuse, then he looked at Blue's sneering red face and decided it was no use. He shrugged and said, 'All right, cobber, if you think that's best.'

'You know it is, boy bach,' the Druid assured him, and thus the two of them lost themselves in the crowd and left the others to find their 'beer and bints'.

Colonel Lyn and Pongo O'Dare didn't feel the same urgency as their men, for they knew that Australia's strict drinking laws didn't apply to them. In the officers' club to which they were heading, they served drinks at virtually any hour. Besides, the two of them didn't need artificial stimulants at the moment. Mountbatten's signal from Ceylon had been short but sweet. It had read, '*Good show. Carry on the good work soonest.*' The message was slightly cryptic but they understood it well enough. They had received the green light. Operation Malay Tiger was definitely on now. All they needed now was a final date for the mission.

Thus it was that Lyn and O'Dare seemed to be walking on air, pushing their way through the GIs who were everywhere, propped up against walls, mindlessly chewing gum, ties askew, overseas caps pushed to the back of their cropped heads, eyeing the whores in a bored fashion, occasionally indicating their intention by jiggling the loose cash in their trouser pockets, which made the whores grin and repeat the routine formula, 'Fancy a good time, Joe?'

Occasionally the big ex-rugger player's attention wandered. But each time Lyn caught his second in command in time with, 'Save it a little longer, Pongo. In the club there will undoubtedly be some English rose willing to sacrifice her all for our brave boys in uniform, and you can be sure *she* won't give you a little present to take home with you.'

And with that Pongo had to be content for the time being . . .

In essence it was the same kind of message that the Druid was trying to pass on to his new friend, the big awkward Aussie nicknamed Horse-arse. But he was not so successful as his beloved CO. 'I ain't much on rock buns and cocoa, Druid,' the ugly-faced aborigine complained. 'Nice of you to bring me along, mate. But a bloke wants more outa life then that, especially if soon he's gonna go into action and probably get his stupid nut blown off.'

The Druid tut-tutted like he'd seen the Reverend Thomas do before the war in the chapel. 'You mustn't think like that, friend,' he chided the much taller Australian. 'I know this is a veritable vale of tears and sorrows, but if we abide by the golden rule, we can come through it safely.'

Horse-arse didn't know what the 'vale of tears and sorrow' was, and even less how you'd survive it by 'abiding by the golden rule'. All he knew was that he had a thirst on him that no Sally Ann cocoa could slake and that his balls itched worse than a bad dose of crabs. 'It's all right for you, Druid,' he mumbled. 'You don't like women—'

The little Welsh medic looked shocked and he opened his mouth to protest, but the other man beat him to it.

'But even if I am half-abo, I still get the urge like the rest of them whiteys. I need a woman. And I've got the money to pay for one.' He slapped his back pocket with a hand like a small steam shovel. He flashed a glance at a big fleshy whore in a short skirt, who swung her bottom from one side to the other flamboyantly as she passed, as if it was worked by some sort of internal metronome. 'Something like that. All that meat and no potatoes!' He laughed wickedly which set the Druid off tut-tutting once again.

'No,' the Druid said sharply. 'It's not right. You're going to get yourself in trouble. Look around you.' He swept his hand around the street packed with GIs and whores. 'What don't you see here –' his face contorted with disgust – 'among all this corruption and the work of the Devil?'

Horse-arse stared at the smaller man in bewilderment. 'What d'yer mean?'

'Well . . .' Now the Druid was embarrassed; he felt he might have gone too far. Still he knew he must attempt to save his comrade from his own weaknesses. 'There are none of the Yanks' black soldiers here, are there? If you follow me, they're not wanted.'

Abruptly the big awkward Australian with the ugly face realized what the Druid was trying to say. 'Strewth, I ain't no nigger! I'm an Australian and my money is as good as any other Aussie.'

'I didn't mean to offend,' the Druid said hastily, but Horse-arse cut him short with, 'I know yer mean well. But you go and scoff your rock buns and the rest o' that church tucker and I'll go and get mesen a woman.' He grinned, showing his misshapen tombstone-like teeth. 'See yer around, cobber.' With that he disappeared into the heaving crowd, leaving the little Welshman to stare after him. He wouldn't see him again.

*　　*　　*

103

The Sydney Officers' Club was unlike any other officers' club that Lyn and Pongo had ever seen. At the door there had been two huge US military policemen in white helmets, carrying white clubs in their hands at the ready, steadily chewing gum like bored ruminating heifers. Neither saluted as the two British officers entered. 'Our cousins from overseas have arrived, I see,' Pongo said in huge good humour.

He was right. Everywhere there were US officers, with smart-looking US Red Cross girls in sky-blue uniforms serving coffee and doughnuts in the foyer, calling out, 'Java and donuts here, gentlemen!' Beyond, an ancient Aussie cleaning woman was sweeping out the ballroom, decorated with blue, white and red flags, where obviously there had been a dance the previous night. Now the tooth-less crone with steel curlers sticking out from beneath her floral turban was holding up a pair of frilly black knickers she had just found and was cackling lecherously.

Pongo grinned. Noting the absence of any sign of the Union flag among all the American bunting and flags, he said, 'Well, Ivan, that's a good sign. It's not only the Union flag that's been pulled down.'

'Shut up,' Lyn hissed as they passed into the dining room, where at the far end there was a group of middle-aged Australian officers stolidly chomping at their food, looking to neither left nor right at the tables crowded with loud talkative American officers. To a slightly amused Lyn they appeared apprehensive, almost as if under siege, being threatened by these brash young Yanks all around them.

Still, he told himself as he and Pongo sat down, soon the young Yanks, mostly infantry officers, would be going to meet their fate in some godforgotten jungle outpost on one of the islands; they deserved a bit of high jinks and fun, however irritating to others, before that happened. They had sudden, violent death written all over their fresh young faces.

He frowned abruptly at the thought and then, dismissing it, concentrated on the food, which he had to admit was a lot better since the Yanks had taken over the catering.

By midday he was quite drunk, not in a loud lolling fashion, but in a happy smiling manner. It seemed to him – still in the club, the bar table aflash with glasses and bottles reflected in the sunlight pouring in through the big window – that all was well with the world. There seemed to be girls everywhere, civilian girls, who shouldn't have been in an officers' club. Not that that worried Lyn. He was happy that they were there. He realized he had grown sick of seeing men all around him with their serious soldierly faces. These tarts, which he supposed they were, pleased him. Even their over-rouged lips and heavily powdered plump faces gave him pleasure. Tarts they might be, all the same, he was happy with them.

Pongo had long departed. Lyn had hardly noticed. His second in command had joked something about 'don't do anything, I wouldn't' and had gone, while he bathed in that pleasant alcoholic haze, enjoying the booze, the sunshine and now the tarts. Some time that afternoon, he told himself idly, before he was too drunk to be capable, he'd take one of the tarts – it didn't matter much which one – up to his room in the club and roger her. He wouldn't be vicious but gentle, even caring. Yes, everything was going well and he had lots of time still. He clicked his fingers at the waiter and ordered another 'chota peg' and then laughed out loud at the look on the man's face. He'd even forgotten what country he was in. This wasn't India, this was Australia!

*　　*　　*

The Druid was lost in more than one sense. He had known he had to get away from the waterfront with its fallen women and drunken servicemen. He'd had enough of that scene of sexual corruption and decadence. But now that he'd ventured away, he felt lost without the sight of the uniforms and military, which had been his world ever since he had been called up back in 1940. Now he found himself in a kind of sleazy seaside suburb with tin-roofed shanties, barefoot bronzed kids in ragged clothes and wooden saloon bars, where they were openly serving great foaming schooners of weak Australian beer illegally to tall rangy men who might have been dockers.

It was not the kind of world the Druid could comprehend. People seemed to be looking at him. The kids ran away at his approach and one of the docker types, drinking ale from a great brown bottle, double the size of beer bottles he remembered from Wales, shouted drunkenly, 'Hop it, Pommy bastard!' and spat in the dust, angry for some reason known only to himself.

Thus it was that the Druid headed for the one place that he recognized and where he might feel at home. For he was hot and thirsty and he felt the need to sit down. At least in the church up ahead, he'd be able to rest in the shade a bit. There might even be a sympathetic pastor he could talk to, though the structure didn't look much like the hill-top chapels he remembered from home. Still, the Druid told himself, perhaps that was the style of Aussie churches in big cities like Sydney.

Blinded after the brightness of the sun outside, the Druid blinked and wrinkled his nose. The interior of the church smelled musty and at the same time sweet: an odour which he couldn't quite identify. Then he had it. It was a mixture of incense and melted wax. His dark face looked alarmed. He was in a Roman Catholic church:

the abode of those evil papists who he knew were little better than the Devil himself. He turned and was about to stumble out again.

Too late. A fat greasy individual in a dirty soutane and stained breviary barred his way. The priest looked, too, as if he might well have been indulging in too much of his own sacramental wine. He beamed at the Druid, revealing gold teeth among the stained diseased ones, and said in a thick accent, 'Welcome, my son . . . Ah, a soldier. You are troubled.' He laid a pudgy hand on the Druid's and added, 'You have come to confess, no doubt, my son. Sins of the flesh as always with you soldiers.' He squeezed the Druid's hand winningly.

The Druid was transfixed with horror. The priest was trying to drag him into some kind of box. He felt the man's evil, stinking breath on his face. He was obviously drunk. That didn't matter now. What mattered was what was he going to do with him in the box.

Again the priest tugged at his hand. 'You can reveal all . . . I understand the temptations of the flesh you poor soldiers are subjected to. *Caro mio.*' Again he gave the Welshman the benefit of that winning smile. 'And afterwards, when I have absolved you, you and I will take a little drink together in my private quarters.' Suddenly the fat priest's smile turned to a knowing leer.

That did it. The Druid pulled himself free from the warm damp hand. Blindly he fled the church, leaving the priest to look after him in absolute bewilderment, muttering in a decidedly sacrilegious manner. '*Porco di Madonna* . . . What I say?'

It was just about then that the Americans killed Horse-arse.

Four

'There were four of them, it appears,' Colonel Lyn said carefully, looking down the ranks of his commandos standing at ease. He had felt that the bad news warranted them standing to attention. But he reasoned that if they had the same kind of hangover that he had, that wouldn't be fair. So he had stood them at ease and now, while they waited for the trucks to take them to the main station, he explained what had happened to the man they had called Horse-arse.

'They were Yanks and they were drunk . . . Like most of us were yesterday. As far as we know from their statements to the US Provost Marshal, they took exception to the fact that our dead comrade was with what they called –' he looked down at the bit of paper he had been given by the authorities – 'a white woman. Though they didn't call her "woman".'

He let his words sink in and most of them looked hangdog and stared down at their boots or scratched themselves, as if it was important to do something, not just stand there. Even Blue, red-eyed and sick-looking, bit his bottom lip.

'Our late comrade didn't like that. Again according to the statements the Yanks made to their military police, the "Aussie nigger got sassy" –' he read the words from his note – 'whatever that means. He told them to go and do something impossible to themselves . . .'

No one smiled.

'Naturally they didn't like it, nor did they like it any more when he, apparently, told them in no uncertain terms to go back to their own country and leave Australia to the Australians like himself. That seemingly did it. One of them tried to punch him, telling him to keep "his goddam coon mouth closed when he spoke to a white man" and they'd only be "too glad to go back home and leave the Aussies to the Nips".'

'I'm sad, but proud of the fact,' Lyn continued, 'that our late comrade fought back. Despite the fact that two of the Yanks arrested were armed with knives and one with some kind of rubber truncheon, he tackled them until –' he stopped and eyed an unhappy Blue who didn't dare meet his gaze – 'one of the Americans ran a knife into his stomach. Then they ran away and left him to die in the gutter . . .' He shrugged and his voice faltered away.

Pongo stepped in. He knew that Horse-arse's death, so shameful and wasteful as it was, had affected the CO. Lyn was a hard man, but the welfare of the troops under his command was paramount; he always felt for them, even when they had gotten themselves into trouble and had been wheeled up in front of him at 'Orders' to be sentenced. Now he barked, his voice sore with all the drinking of the day before, 'Troop . . . Troop – *attenshun!*'

As one, fifty-odd pairs of heavy, steel-shod ammunition boots slammed down on the concrete and the men stood rigidly to attention, their eyes fixed on some distant horizon. Up from behind the station, a battered old pre-war cab was heading in their direction, with a civilian leaning out of the off-side window crying, 'Hang on there, gentlemen . . . Hang on . . . *Sydney Herald* here . . .'

Pongo ignored the civilian. He cried in his best parade-ground voice, 'Corporal Jenkins, please take over!'

Corporal Jenkins, well known for his love of drill and what the Aussies of the commando called 'Pommy bullshite', stepped forward smartly. He did a beautiful about turn and cried, 'Off–icer on pa–rade. Salute . . . Dis–miss!'

As one, the men turned to their left, raised their hands to their bush hats in salute and marched a couple of paces away before relaxing, letting their shoulders slump, one or two of them farting, as if with relief, and coming to a stop next to their heaped kit.

It was then that a middle-aged civilian in a rumpled suit that looked far too thick for the Australian climate, with an old-fashioned watch chain decorating his well-filled waistcoat, approached and said in an accent which was more cockney than Australian, 'Hey cobbers, which of you gents is Colonel Lyn?'

The CO turned, a little surprised. 'I am. Why do you ask?'

'It's about the abo who's been murdered by the Yanks,' the civilian said, displaying a mouthful of bad teeth. 'Like to ask you a few questions, Colonel. Won't take half a mo.' He pulled out a notebook and a stub of pencil. He licked the end of the pencil and poised it there above the pad, obviously ready for business. 'Now then, what's the name of this abo that the Yanks croaked?'

Hastily Lyn held up his hands. 'I can't answer any of your questions,' he countered. 'You'd better talk to Army Command HQ if you want that kind of information.'

'Come off it, Colonel,' the man from the *Sydney Herald* said easily, in no way put off by Lyn's reaction. 'You know them toffee-nosed brass hats. They wouldn't give yer the muck from beneath their fingernails. Besides, the

Yanks – and MacArthur – are bearing down on 'em hard. They don't want any more nasty stories getting out about the Yanks in Aussie.' He licked the end of his pencil once more, as if he was only too eager to get on with the job and felt he was being held up by useless chat. 'Think the frigging Yanks was occupying Aussie instead of being here as our allies.'

Pongo grinned and told himself that the fat, middle-aged civilian wasn't exactly an old Etonian. Perhaps his editor cleaned up his grammatical mistakes.

Lyn sighed, as if his patience was being sorely tried. 'I've told you, sir, that I am not empowered to give out any information. You'll just have to take it up with headquarters.'

The reporter looked at him as if he was seeing the tall bronzed officer for the first time. 'Don't get shirty with me, Colonel. After all, you are a Pom, and the Aussies don't like Poms much either.'

Lyn thought it better to ignore the civilian. He turned to Corporal Jenkins, who was standing by, looking utterly rigid in his 'at-ease' pose, hands clasped behind his ramrod-straight back. 'Corporal, will you see this – er – gentleman back to his taxi.'

'Sir!' Jenkins barked, stamping his right foot down as if he were back on the barracks square at the depot in England. He did a perfect about turn and faced the much smaller cockney. 'All right, mate,' he snapped out of the side of his thin-lipped mouth, which looked as if it were worked with tight-furled steel springs. 'Hop it!'

The reporter wasn't impressed. 'You can't talk to me that way, Corporal. You don't know the power of—'

He never finished the sentence. 'Can't I?' Jenkins said. His big hands lashed out. One grabbed the civilian by the back of his greasy collar, the other by the seat of his baggy pants. In a flash Jenkins had lifted the civilian off his feet and was frog-marching him back to where the grinning taxi-driver had opened the cab door with a great flourish, obviously highly amused at the whole business.

Jenkins dumped the civilian in the back and wiped his big hands together, as if he had touched something very dirty. 'OK, on yer way, mate, and let's get on with the war.'

'Fuck the war!' the reporter gasped, his fat face a dangerous-looking puce colour. 'What's yer bloody name, Corporal?'

''Itler . . . Corporal Adolf Hitler.'

The taxi-driver chuckled. 'That's a good 'un, cobber,' he said and, seeing the fun was about over, swung himself behind the wheel of the pre-war Australian Ford and turned on the engine.

'Mind yer fingers,' Jenkins said and slammed the rear door closed.

The reporter seemed ready to explode at any minute. 'Don't think you're gonna get away with this, mate. Cos you ain't. I'll fix your heels, you Pommy baskits.'

'You and whose frigging army?' Jenkins sneered, and then the taxi was driving off, with the red-faced reporter still waving his fat fist out of the rear window.

Corporal Jenkins wasn't impressed. 'Civvies!' he said to no one in particular. 'I've shat 'em for breakfast.' Then, swinging his arms proudly, he marched to where the others were waiting.

Book Four

The Mission Commences

One

C olonel Tanaka of the Singapore Kemptai was a little drunk and angry, as usual. He was dressing for the interview with that damned Christian from Nagasaki, who he guessed was after his job, and despite the Scotch, he was taking care with his appearance. He stared at his hairless upper body in the mirror on the wall before he drew on the immaculate white starched shirt and told himself he was still a fine figure. Admittedly he was a bit heavy around the waist, but he had the shoulders and thighs of a professional boxer, such as the ones he had seen in those Yankee movies before the war. Why, any woman should be honoured to go to bed with a man like that.

He frowned, took another drink from the neck of the Scotch bottle and then wiped his thick, dark-red lips. Why, he asked his image in the mirror, could he not experience that rapturous explosion of blood and passion that was the due of every red-blooded man? *Why?*

He groaned. Some of his friends and cronies in the mess had suggested powdered rhino horn or Siberian tiger tooth and he had spent a small fortune with those damned Chink medic men. To no avail. Others had come up with garlic. He had wolfed the stuff down by the kilo until his breath could have felled a sumo wrestler at twenty paces – all three hundred pounds of fat and muscle. The garlic had not worked, just as oysters, stinging nettles, whips and all the rest of the supposed remedies hadn't.

He groaned again and slowly, miserably, pulled on his shirt. He had tried everything and still he had been unable to savour those tremendously exciting pleasures that were the birthright of every upstanding Japanese officer. Even now when he could have had any woman he wanted – Chinese, Eurasian, even white ones (they were all imprisoned in Kemptai prisons with absolutely no rights whatsoever) – he couldn't get that craved-for erection.

He strapped on his sword belt. Instinctively his hand went to his pistol holster, with the comforting stiff heavy weight of the pistol it contained. For a moment or two he felt reassured that things would work out and that he would regain his lost potency: the thing uppermost in his mind, more important than the fate of the Emperor himself.

In the interrogation room beyond the wall he could hear the muted cries and sobs of a woman. He knew what was going on in there. His men would be sexually abusing one of the female prisoners. Whether it was for their own amusement or to obtain information, he neither knew nor cared. All that suddenly interested him was that those stupid peasants, who had spent their early lives standing in the shit of the rice paddies, could now enjoy women of all classes and races. He, for his part, could enjoy nothing.

Now he could hear the woman's breath coming in fast, hectic gasps. He didn't need a crystal ball to guess what his men were doing to her now. They'd have her on the table, legs strapped high and wide, with each of them straddling her in turn and thrusting their filthy peasant dicks into that beautiful wet orifice, making her pant with pain – and perhaps pleasure too.

He howled with the sheer misery of it all. His breath was coming in shallow gasps, as if he were in there straddling the unknown woman, thrusting himself into her like he had done the Manchurian whores in what now seemed like another age. Abruptly he realized he had taken the pistol out of its holster, was fondling its hard tumescence. He choked. Hastily he thrust the pistol away. What was wrong with him? Was he going mad? Why was he carrying on like this, a loyal servant of His Majesty, whose private affairs were of nothing in the light of the Japanese mission to bring peace, prosperity and Nippon's power to these unenlightened fellow Asiatics?

'You bastard!' he cried drunkenly at his image in the big mirror on the wall. 'You self-centred, perverted bastard . . . For God's sake, pull yourself together!'

He finished his dressing, took a final swig from the litre bottle of Scotch, splashed some cold water on his burning cheeks and went up to the outer office where Kimura had been waiting for him for some time. But then he had expected that. Senior Japanese officers of Colonel Tanaka's type always made their subordinates wait; it was part of the ritual.

Kimura bowed low.

Tanaka bowed too, but not so low. He indicated a seat and, sitting down himself, grunted. 'Well, Lieutenant, where's the fire?'

'It has not started yet, sir.'

'Don't be funny,' Tanaka snapped grumpily. 'Get on with it. Why do you want to see me? I have other things to do than listen to the silly fantasies of junior officers.'

The lieutenant's face revealed nothing. He was used to being humiliated by these dinosaurs. But his day would come and then the dear Colonel Tanaka would be in for a surprise. 'I have worked out several things since I last saw you, sir, and have come to certain conclusions which I think might interest you, sir.'

'Don't be so shitting pompous, Lieutenant,' Tanaka scoffed. He took out one of the long Russian *paparossi* that he favoured and lit it. He didn't offer one to the other officer. The lieutenant coughed at the strong black Maroka tobacco. It pleased Tanaka. The damned Christian couldn't even stand the odour of strong tobacco. Typical of those types.

Kimura waited. He had all the patience in the world. In essence, he knew, with his clear analytical mind trained by those Jesuit priests back home, who had worked hard to remove all traces of Japanese irrationality from his brain, that he was engaged in a battle with his superior. It was a kind of minor war between two people of the same race. He waged it, not to humiliate Tanaka, but for the sake of Japan. People like Tanaka with their silly bushido irrational way of thinking, believing essentially what they wanted to believe, would lose the war for Japan. It was his task to stop them, if he could.

The Tanakas of the Imperial Japanese forces had won this new Empire for Japan since 1941. But it was people like himself who would keep it intact and beat their Anglo-American enemies, growing more powerful by the week and month, with logical thinking.

'Colonel,' he began again. 'I have formed the opinion that the British and the Australians will attempt to raid Singapore.'

That shook Tanaka, as Kimura had anticipated it would. This was no mealy-mouthed crawling humble subordinate-to-superior kind of statement. This was direct, straight to the point, the way the Jesuit teachers back home would have commenced an argument.

'What did you say, Kimura?'

He repeated his words.

'How?' Now it seemed that Tanaka was reduced, too, to bald unemotional expressions Kimura hoped Tanaka would continue in that manner. It would make things easier.

'It is like a mosaic, Colonel. I have certain pieces and I put them together to produce a pattern, which I hope is a rational one.' He shrugged and then, knowing how Tanaka wished always to be respected for his rank, bowed and added, 'First, I have the transcript of a meeting in Ceylon between Lord Mountbatten and his generals. Lord Mountbatten is—'

'I know who Mountbatten is,' Tanaka interrupted, interested now. 'Get on with it.'

'Colonel. Well, one of our spies heard something of an operation called Operation Malay Tiger.'

Tanaka nodded, but didn't interrupt this time.

'Good, now we can add something to that. A little time before that, one of his Majesty's –' he drew in his breath as a sign of respect, while opposite him Tanaka bowed at the mention of the Imperial name – 'destroyers was sunk while attacking an enemy submarine. However, as this submarine crash-dived, there must have been some of the enemy planning a mission on the deck. In their haste to get away, they left certain objects on the deck, which our people managed to collect before the – er – unfortunate incident.' He fumbled in the briefcase which he had brought with him from Naval Intelligence and then carefully withdrew the papers that had been dried out and had now become crumbly. 'These documents.' He passed them over to Tanaka, who naturally couldn't read English, but who made a great show of surveying them, as if he could. 'As you can see,' he added, feeling an absolute hypocrite, 'and can – er – read for yourself,

Colonel, they show that an operation was planned or *is* planned against Singapore. You see the title, "Operation Jaycock".'

Tanaka mumbled something.

Lieutenant Kimura let him off the hook. The situation was too grave to make fun of the fat perverted fool at this moment. 'As I have said, pieces of the mosaic, which have to be fitted together to make some sense. A crossword puzzle in other words.'

Now that Tanaka knew the direction the damned Christian was taking, he felt confident enough to snap, 'Don't test my patience, Kimura. I haven't got all the time in the world, you know.'

'Sir. One final piece of the jigsaw and then, with your kind permission, I will explain what I think the enemy is about. The *Sydney Herald*, sir. It is an Australian paper. We got this from our friend, the Spanish consul —'

'You mean the fellow you *bribe*. He's no friend. But continue . . .' He waved a podgy hand in the younger officer's direction.

'Well, sir, I won't bore you with the details. It concerns the killing of an Australian soldier by an American.' Kimura paused, as if he expected a reaction. None came and he went on. 'However, would you take a look at the picture which accompanies the article. It says the man is the officer in charge of the unit to which the dead Australian belonged. It is not very good, but clear enough, I hope, sir.' He passed the paper across.

Tanaka finished his cigarette deliberately, taking his time, showing the Christian who was master here. Finally he stubbed out the wooden stem of the Russian cigarette and deigned to look at the piece, his fat yellow face the perfect picture of boredom.

Obviously the photo of the English officer in his green

beret had been taken covertly, that much he knew. It was blurred and was taken from the front, while the Englishman had been unbuttoning his shirt for some reason; perhaps he was too hot. At his foot there was a heavy pack upon which was balanced a tommy gun. Perhaps, again, the man had taken off his kit to relieve himself of the weight on a very hot day. In the background he could see the round ball of the sun. He pursed his thick lips, wondering what Kimura expected him to see; for he couldn't spot anything of significance about the poor-quality snapshot. Finally he gave up. He dropped the paper on his desk and said, 'Well, what is of such great importance, Kimura? I see nothing.'

Kimura allowed himself a careful smile. He had known that Tanaka was too stupid to put the pieces of the mosaic together. Sometimes he wondered how in three devils' names the fat colonel had ever got into Kemptai intelligence. Influential friends in Tokyo, he supposed. 'Those three pieces mean the following, Colonel.' He raised his carefully manicured left hand and then with his right ticked off the points. '*One*, with the documents washed overboard from the English submarine and captured by Naval Intelligence was the name of the officer in command of this Operation Jaywick. It was Colonel I. Lyn. *Two*, the name of the operation mentioned by Lord Mountbatten at that dinner in Ceylon was Operation Malay Tiger—'

'Yes, yes,' Tanaka snapped in irritation, 'I am not yet senile! I remember.'

'Well, sir, *three* –' as if by magic he produced a magnifying glass and handed it to a surprised Colonel Tanaka – 'if you will look at that officer's chest, you will be able to recognize the tattoo upon him, I am sure.' He smiled, again very carefully, for Kimura knew he must not let Tanaka dismiss the results of all this work in one of his foolish blind rages.

Intrigued in spite of his intense dislike of the Christian, he took the glass and stared at the English officer. A tiger's head leapt into the centre of the gleaming glass. From it radiated a few stripes. 'It's a tiger,' Tanaka said stupidly.

'Yessir!' Now Kimura couldn't contain himself. 'A Malay tiger, by the stripes, I have been told. Obviously this Englishman – I. Lyn – once served in Malaya, where he had the tattoo done. But most importantly, sir, Mountbatten's reference and this tattoo connect Operation Malay Tiger, Operation Jaywick and this man.' He licked his dry lips hastily. 'I conclude that this Colonel Lyn conducted an operation against Singapore, which we took for native sabotage carried out from the port itself, and plans a new operation called after this, his own tattoo – Operation Malay Tiger . . .' He faltered and his words faded away to nothing.

For what seemed an eternity the two men froze there, the only sounds the faint whimper of the woman being tortured in the interrogation room and the soft whirr of the overhead fan. Finally Tanaka said softly, for he was impressed by his subordinate's clever detective work, 'The tattoo links this colonel to an old operation and a new one planned by Mountbatten?'

'Yessir.'

'I believe you, Kimura. Now the question is where the English are going to strike this time?'

Kimura didn't hesitate. He had been praying for this question all along. '*Singapore* again, sir!'

Two

'*When that man is dead and gone,*' the half-naked sailor sang softly, white cap perched at the back of his head, '*some fine day the news will flash. Satan with a small moustache is asleep beneath the lawn . . . When that man is dead and gone . . .*' The sailor paused in his song and dabbed another lick of paint on the *Porpoise*'s now camouflaged hull. For soon she would be sailing and the skipper had decided to adopt the camouflage used by Jap submarines.

'Wish that bugger'd shut up,' Blue growled.

'Wish they'd stand us down and I could go and have a piss. I'm bursting for a jimmy riddle,' the next man in the ranks groaned.

And Corporal Jenkins, as regimental as ever, despite the heat and the fact that they were leaving that day, snapped, 'Stop that talking in the ranks there! What d'yer think this is – the frigging Pioneer Corps!'

Someone in the rear rank farted loudly and Jenkins glared in that direction, muttering, 'And none of yer frigging dumb insolence. I'll have the next man who does that inside quicker than his bleeding plates o' meat can touch the bleeding ground!'

But the troopers waiting in the hot sun for the CO to address them weren't moved. They knew that Corporal Jenkins wouldn't be putting anybody 'inside' for a long time now. The sailor, fifty yards away on the submarine, seemed to realize that, too, for now he changed his tune to the old soldiers' ditty about 'saying good-bye to 'em all, the long and the short and the tall . . . Yer'll get no promotion on this side of the ocean . . . so cheer up me lads, fuck 'em all!'

Standing under the only tree in the area, enjoying the shade, for there was not even a breath of a wind coming from the mirror-like gleaming surface of the sea, Pongo told himself that the men were in good heart. They knew what they were going into, but no one had tried to dodge the mission by going sick or deserting. They were all in it, however dangerous Operation Malay Tiger might turn out to be. It was good to know that these chaps, bronzed and top-fit after the last week of intensive training, could be relied upon even in the tightest corner.

Over on the submarine they had stowed away the last of the Sleeping Beauties. Now with the rest of their kits already loaded, the *Porpoise* could sail on time, just after nightfall. Air reconnaissance and the code-breakers, who regularly read the Japanese naval code, had reported no enemy naval action in their area. All the same, Commander Marsham, the skipper of the *Porpoise*, was not going to take the slightest risk. As he had told Lyn and Pongo earlier that day, 'You and your boys are the ones who are going to grip the dirty end of the stick. I'm just your bus driver. But I'm going to ensure that you get there safely all right.' It was something which both the Army officers could appreciate and despite the earliness of the hour, they had toasted the success of their mission with a pink gin. Indeed, as Pongo now recalled, they had done in several pink gins. For, in these last hours, the CO had relaxed a little and had allowed the chaps to have 'one last decent piss-up', as he had put it the night before. Some, Pongo could see, were still suffering as a result. His grin broadened and he told himself he'd ensure that the gin didn't run out till they reached their forward base at Merapas. Thereafter, there'd be no more time for pink gin.

Now Colonel Lyn came striding purposefully from his tent, a chart under his right arm. Behind him trotted the Druid like a pet dog, holding a large brown bottle. Pongo's grin vanished immediately when he saw it. He knew what the bottle contained and why and he didn't like the idea one bit. For a moment he wished the CO hadn't hit upon the idea of giving the stuff to the chaps. But he supposed that Lyn's intention was honourable, giving the chaps a chance to make their own decisions like that. All the same, he didn't like it; he didn't think that it was good for the men's morale. Then he decided he'd better get on parade, too. Everyone was in this, whatever the outcome of Operation Malay Tiger might be. There could be no exceptions, even for officers. Lightly for such a big man, he ran to join the rest.

Swiftly Corporal Jenkins called the troop to attention. Colonel Lyn, with the Druid and his bottle standing behind, acknowledged the corporal's salute and stood the parade at ease. Immediately he got down to business. 'I'm not going to waste many more words, chaps,' he said, his face glistening with sweat, for it was a hot afternoon. 'I think most of what has to be said has been said. What I'd like to say now is threefold. First I'd like to thank you all for your steadfastness and reliability. You've stood up to some damned tough training successfully. Secondly, you know what the success of our mission will mean. Not only will we sink Jap shipping, but we'll also give a boost to the morale of our lads fighting on the frontier with India. In addition, we hope we'll cheer up our poor fellows who are incarcerated in those Jap hell camps. They'll know we're fighting to release them one day.' Lyn stopped and looked along their ranks, as if trying to fix each and every one of their faces in his mind for ever.

His look was so piercing and intense that Pongo felt the urge to look away. But he didn't. For some reason he couldn't explain then or during the rest of his short life, he felt he had to meet that look; it was part of some secret, almost mystical bond between them and the CO.

'Third,' Lyn said after a moment, 'there is one last thing.' He indicated that the Druid should come closer. 'I hope this will never happen and I know I shall do my damnedest to see that it doesn't. But if it does, I want you to spare yourselves unnecessary suffering and brutality. If we have to leave anyone behind because he is severely wounded or if there is a danger that you will fall into Jap hands – and all of you know what the Japs will do with any prisoner – I want you to swallow the L-Pill.'

'L-Pill, sir?' Blue blurted out.

Corporal Jenkins flashed the big Australian a killing look and opened his mouth to tell him to keep silent in the ranks, but Lyn stopped him with, 'Lethal – L for lethal, Blue.' He used the Australian's nickname for the first time since the latter had joined the unit. 'A suicide pill, in other words,' he added very quietly.

Pongo frowned. Now it was out and a sudden silence descended upon the little parade, as if the men were realizing for the very first time what they had let themselves in for. Lyn nodded to the Druid. The Druid nodded back. He unscrewed the cap of the brown bottle and then, passing from man to man, silently handed them the pill that could mean the sudden difference between life and death. In equal silence each man accepted the L-Pill and swiftly hid it away without looking down at it, as if they didn't want to be reminded of its purpose.

Two hours later the *Porpoise* sailed for Merapas island. Just before the Australian coast finally disappeared into the darkness, Pongo and Colonel Lyn took a turn on deck with the permission of Commander Marsham, the *Porpoise*'s skipper. The naval officer knew how difficult it was for these 'brown jobs' to get used to long hours confined in a submarine below the sea. He felt, therefore, he could break regulations a little to let them have some extra time on deck.

Now slowly the two of them paced back and forth between the big submarine's deck gun and the conning tower, thinking more than they were saying. For they were in a strange mood. Naturally they had been on these sorts of missions before. But neither of the big hard men had experienced the kind of sombre sense of foreboding which they were experiencing now. Perhaps it was caused by the fact the CO had handed out the L-Pill for the first time. Perhaps it was something else that neither of them could rationalize.

So they walked and talked sporadically about what amounted really to nothing. In the end they both seemed glad when Commander Marsham called from the conning tower, 'Time's up, gentlemen. I'm going to order dive stations in half a mo.' Behind them the coast of Australia disappeared finally into the night. Neither of them looked back.

The next two days passed in the usual boring cramped routine of the submarine, in which the air grew increasingly foul by the hour. As Blue complained more than once, 'It stinks like one great big fart all the time. It puts a digger off his tucker.' In his case it didn't. But the atmosphere did have an effect on the other 'brown jobs' eating habits, so that most of them could only eat their suppers when finally the conning tower hatch was flung open and the fresh keen night air flooded the fetid, stinking interior for a little while. As the *Porpoise* cruised on the surface and recharged her electric batteries, they breathed in clean air.

Mostly, however, they sat on the cramped bunks, too listless to play housey-housey or read letters from their loved ones, dozing off all the time until the other watch came down to claim their beds. A couple of times, Lyn thought he'd get them busy checking their equipment: the usual sort of thing, sharpening commando knives, unloading Bren magazines and cleaning the bullets, oiling the firing mechanisms of their tommy guns and the like. But he could see their hearts weren't in it and finally he gave up. He told himself that all that sort of thing could be done at Merapas.

The island was located in the Java Sea some seventy miles from Singapore, just the right distance for the new secret weapon. The island was thought to be uninhabited and, if it was, that meant the Japs could have no reason to land there, or even run patrols by boat to it.

From the island, where they would land their stores, they would sail out into the area to find a native craft, a junk, a sampan or even a large prau, anything large enough to take the Sleeping Beauties and their crews. Then it was planned they would sneak into the Singapore harbour area and carry out their daring mission. As Colonel Lyn had remarked more than once to his second in command, 'There are plenty of ifs in the plan, Pongo. But we were lucky last time and I don't see why we shouldn't be this time.' Pongo had agreed, but if Lyn hadn't been so preoccupied with his plan, he would have noticed that Pongo didn't exhibit his usual hearty confidence.

So, while the *Porpoise* ploughed steadily through what appeared to be empty seas, Lyn told himself he'd shelve everything till they reached the island in the Java Sea. Once they arrived at Merapas everything would fall into place, he was confident of that. But in the heads, the submarine's tight little lavatory, the only place in the *Porpoise* where he could be alone and not subject to the ridicule and jeers of the others, the Druid started to pray more fervently than ever; and Blue, when he thought the others weren't looking, would take his L-Pill from the matchbox in which he kept it and stare at it. Thoughts of a kind that he had never experienced before would animate his rough, uneducated face and once there came tears of what appeared to be self-pity in his eyes, as if he had realized something about himself which had made him sad. Once, when he was overcome by these strange unusual moods, he had murmured to himself, 'Time is running out.'

Lying naked on the next bunk with just a washcloth across his bare genitals, a half-asleep Corporal Jenkins had queried, 'Running out, Blue? What?'

'You must have heard me wrong, Corp,' Blue replied, a guilty look flashing across his face abruptly. 'Go back to kip.' And with that he had thrust his pill back in the box and hastily hidden it in his pocket.

Three

Lieutenant Kimura took out his handkerchief with his white-gloved hand and mopped his sweat-damp face with it. He had doused it with perfume just before he had left his quarters and he hoped the perfume might cover any smell he gave off. But it was not the sticky heat of a late Singapore afternoon which made him sweat so heavily; it was nervous tension at the prospect of meeting her. Why, he had not only donned his number one uniform with its stiff white collar, but he also wore a sword, which he disliked doing. He felt he looked foolish imitating those so-called samurai warriors like his chief, Colonel Tanaka. Most of them were damned peasants anyway, with the pig shit still clinging to their heels. Besides, he didn't feel, as a practising Christian, he should carry such a barbarian, un-Christian weapon.

No, it wasn't the heat which made him sweat as he stood a little helplessly outside the Girls' Superior Christian Academy, waiting for the bell to ring and the nuns to release their pupils. It was the thought that this afternoon she would walk with him to a café in the Japanese quarter where he would buy her tea and sticky rice buns and, if she wished, one of the place's expensive water ices that came in so many garish colours. But he expected well-born girls of her type and young years would like such things. He hoped so. For really up to now his experiences with women had been limited to whores, one time, when he had been really desperate for a female, with one of the low-born Korean women who acted as comfort girls. After sex with her – and my God, wasn't she ugly like all those damned Korean women? – he had stood under a shower for nearly an hour and then applied the usual unguents to his sexual organs in case she had given him one of those terrible diseases. For days afterwards he had been preoccupied examining his penis for the first sign of a red sore and discharge which would have indicated the worst.

Iris, as she had told him he could call her when they were alone, was totally different. She was a Eurasian, of course, but she favoured her Japanese mother. Any Japanese who observed her delicate features and upswept jet-black hair in a casual fashion would not have noticed any difference between her and the smart young women one found in the streets of Tokyo. Only under closer scrutiny might the observer have remarked on the fact that her legs were not bowed as they were so often in Japanese girls and that she was taller. That indicated a European father. In her case, as she had told him a little sadly, a German trader who had been killed during the siege of Singapore two years before.

She was a Christian, of course, like himself. That was what had first attracted him to her. Naturally he desired her sexually. It would not have been natural if he hadn't. More than once he had visualized her naked: a slim pale body with tiny breasts, tipped pink and very virginal, and just the faintest fuzz of dark pubic hair so that he was able to see the little red slit beneath. It had excited him. But he had controlled himself. There were always whores who would do that kind of thing for him for a handful of yen. No, he liked her for her demure looks, her intelligence, even superiority, which he supposed came a little from her dead German father. Why, he could even take her so seriously that he might write to his father, the high-school teacher in Nagasaki, and tell him of her. He wondered what his honourable parent would think if he wrote that he was thinking of marrying his Iris.

His pleasant thoughts were interrupted by the tinkle of the school bell, the rope pulled from the outside of the main building by a burly nun in a great white headdress. The 'white swan', as Iris said they called the nuns, looked, he told himself, like a wrestler with her brawny bare arms and trace of a moustache. Then there Iris was, with a group of the other girls, books in a strap over her shoulder, dressed in pure white, laughing and giggling in the silly fashion teenage girls had. He swallowed hard and felt himself begin to sweat even more. Wasn't she pretty? Much too pretty for him.

Suddenly she saw him. He clicked to attention and, bowing slightly, raised his gloved hand to his cap. He ventured a smile. But the laughter had frozen on her face. He smiled more broadly. As if she was making a conscious effort to do so, she relaxed and said something hastily to the others. They were all Eurasians like herself, save one big blonde girl with large feet, very plain, who he suspected might have been English or American. It didn't matter. He was concentrating solely on Iris.

Iris looked around, probably to check whether any of the German nuns were watching her. They weren't. She raised a finger to her lips, as if in warning to the other girls. They giggled even more and then she was running lightly towards the gate, her breasts jigging up and down beautifully under her tight white blouse.

'God in Heaven!' he cursed to himself. He had begun to sweat yet more heavily. He prayed he wouldn't smell.

She came to a halt a few feet from him, not even breathing hard. She bowed slightly and flashed him a white-toothed perfect smile. His heart leapt to his throat. He clutched the hilt of his sword tightly and said in a strained voice, 'It is a pleasant day, Miss Iris.' He spoke English, as she did when they were together.

'It is pleasant indeed,' she echoed, as if repeating a lesson. 'And how are you today, Lieutenant Kimura? Well, I hope?'

'Yes, exceedingly well, thank you.' Now she had fallen in step next to him, ignoring the grins and pointed looks of a truckload of Japanese Army fatigue men passing. He flashed them a hard glance. They looked away immediately. No one wanted to get involved with the dreaded Kemptai.

For a while they continued the stilted conversation in English. Now and then he ventured to hold her arm as he steered her through the vendors selling sizzling fish heads and bean curd in peanut oil, as if he were afraid that the pungent odour might taint her fragile Eurasian beauty. Once, he stepped boldly into the path of a Japanese truck laden with drunken soldiers returning to their troopship – who were urinating over the side of the vehicle – and held it up. The driver, perhaps drunk himself, stepped on the brakes in time. Sternly the young officer, hand held on the hilt of his sword, ordered them to cease immediately. The look on his face told the happy infantrymen he was not fooling. They stuffed their organs back in their breeches and those who couldn't help themselves continued urinating on their boots. He waved the truck on with his features set in a martial look.

She raised her gaze demurely as the truck drove off and said in passable, rather quaint Japanese, 'Oh, Lieutenant, you are so masterful.'

133

He allowed himself a smile and didn't notice the half-naked coolie on the rusty Raleigh bicycle who had appeared out of the traffic suddenly and pretending to test his worn tyre, was gazing at them intently. 'They are not bad men. But they are soldiers. And soldiers must have their fun before they die for our flag and our Emperor.' He drew his breath in sharply as a mark of great respect.

'But you will not die, Lieutenant Kimura.'

He shrugged slightly and said, 'I hope not.'

'But you are of the Kemptai. They do not fight.'

He did not feel insulted by the remark. Instead he was flattered that she had noticed he was in the secret police, though he did not ask how a schoolgirl would recognize the Kemptai insignia. All that he told himself was that she was interested in him and his welfare. That was a good sign. He said, 'Do you think I could invite you for tea and some cakes, young lady?' Again he spoke English.

She gave a kind of curtsy and her delicate breasts trembled delightfully once more under the tight silk blouse. He swallowed hard and felt himself blushing. How desirable she was!

Behind them, as they entered the café, which smelled of burned almonds and scented Chinese tea, the coolie on the Raleigh bicycle swung his long leg over the crossbar once more. 'Jap cunt,' he said under his breath. 'Now she's got yer . . .' And with that he disappeared into the crowded noisy street . . .

It was that night that the signal was received at Supreme Headquarters' Decode-and-Decipher Office, which was then flashed by Ultra to MacArthur's HQ in Australia, where it was noted and filed away for future reference. It read: 'Two main Kemptai officers, Singapore, identified.' There followed brief references to Colonel Tanaka and

Lieutenant Kimura, with a few details of their military background, which the SOE planning officers weren't particularly interested in, though they did remark on the thoroughness of their unpaid helpers in Singapore.

What the SOE planners were interested in, however, was how they could fit the two Japs into the forth-coming operation. They knew that Mountbatten wanted the maximum publicity for Operation Malay Tiger, if it was successful; and one thing that would help to ensure success, they concluded, was to bamboozle Jap intelligence. 'Throw a bit o' sand in their eyes, what, chaps,' as one of them remarked in the hearty voice of a regular officer who planned the murder of his fellow human beings every morning before breakfast and didn't think twice about it. In fact, he was a pale-faced ex-Oxford don, who had taught Sanskrit and had led an exemplary and absolutely harmless life out at Upper Heyford before he had been – very much to his surprise – called up. 'I mean, chaps, get rid of them just before the op is due to commence.'

'Get rid of them?' Sandy, who often wore ladies' lingerie in the privacy of his own quarters of a Saturday night – it was his customary weekend treat – queried. 'How do you mean, old sport?'

By way of an answer, the ex-reader in Sanskrit drew a finger across his throat.

'Gosh, Tiger,' Sandy breathed in awe. '*That!*'

Tiger nodded solemnly.

Some time that same night, the signal, coded at the highest level, went out to that half-naked coolie with the rusty old Raleigh bike in Singapore. It was brief and quite brutal. It read: '*Liquidate targets – soonest.*' There was no signature. Not even a pair of initials. Naturally,

135

Sandy and the ex-reader in Sanskrit would not like to have a murder – or would assassination sound better? – on their records or conscience when they returned to the teacups, bath olivers and the classy chats about the world of those dreamy spires, would they now . . . ?

Four

N ow the sun had started to slip beyond the horizon at last. Dark shadows like giant prehistoric birds began to race across the still waters of the Java Sea. Almost at once, as the evening sky flushed a last dramatic red, the heat diminished. Crouched low in the lead Sleeping Beauty, Colonel Lyn wiped his arm across his brow. Now he could see without the beads of perspiration dripping into his eyes. 'Thank God,' he whispered to no one in particular.

He gave the signal. Silently, like grey ghosts, the two craft began to slip through the glowing tropical sea. Behind him, Jenkins did the work of steering while the big commando colonel concentrated on the shore of the island. Now, in the last of the light, he could just see the strip of white beach, surrounded by the thick mangrove swamps which reached down to it. But a portion was clear. It would be there, he decided, that they would land the supplies from the *Porpoise*, which was way out in the bay – if everything was clear. On present count, Lyn told himself, it seemed the island was as deserted as Intelligence had stated it was.

Behind them Blue and the Druid, bringing up the signal lights, kept a safe distance of some fifty yards. If anything happened to the lead boat, it would be their job to warn off the others. Then Lyn and Jenkins would be on their own.

Instinctively the colonel felt for his L-Pill, which he had concealed in the lining of the collar of his bush shirt.

They came closer. Now Lyn could just see the faint white line of the gentle surf. 'Turn off the engine, Corporal,' he commanded. 'We'll glide in.'

'Sir!' Jenkins barked.

Lyn frowned. The corporal was far too regimental for the commandos really. He always spoke in a loud tone as if he were back on some UK barracks square, drilling raw recruits. Still, he was a good man; they all were. Head cocked to one side, tensed for the slightest sound, Lyn readied himself for the landing. Behind him, Jenkins pulled out the silenced Sten gun: another secret weapon that Mountbatten had granted them. Yet somehow Lyn felt he wouldn't need it. For, apart from the usual jungle noises, there was no other sound coming from the island of Merapas.

Carefully the two of them, well spread out, their weapons at the ready, waded through the bright white surf heading for the dark mystery of the beach and the mangroves beyond. Somewhere a bird was shrieking. It was answered by some sort of monkey that sounded to a tense Lyn like a crazy man shouting his head off. He realized that, thanks to his months of training in the jungle, such strange noises didn't upset him. It was different from the average Tommy, a town dweller who would be terrified when confronted by such a racket at night in enemy territory.

They came to the beach. Lyn screwed up his eyes and peered to left and right. Nothing. No sign of footprints on the sand. He nodded to Jenkins and indicated to the right. Jenkins gripped his silenced Sten gun and nodded back. Lyn cast a glance behind him. Pongo and the Druid came a little closer to the beach. In the front of the Sleeping Beauty, the big ex-rugby player gripped the flare pistol more tightly with a hand that was wet with sweat. If anything went wrong, he would fire it and then signal the *Porpoise*. He knew it was against Lyn's orders but he wasn't going to leave the boss to the mercy of the Japs if there were any on the island. *No sir!*

The two leading commandos disappeared into the mangroves. It was wet and muddy under foot and they had their work cut out trying to dodge the muddier bits and thus make less noise. All the same a worried Lyn felt they could probably be heard all the way to Singapore, the racket they were making. But after a while the swamp started to give way to what was a banana plantation that had been allowed to run wild.

'It looks as if Intelligence got it wrong,' Lyn said softly, as they crouched on the edge of the place viewing a derelict hut that now housed rats – they could hear them scuttling claw-footed in the straw of the holed roof quite clearly.

'Ay, sir,' Jenkins added stolidly. He wasn't an imaginative man. He seemed to take everything in his stride. 'Shall we get on with the recce, sir?'

Lyn grinned in the warm gloom. Nothing would shake Jenkins. 'Yes, let's get on with it.'

They passed through the banana plantation without incident and already they could hear the hiss-and-slither of the surf on the other side of the island. Obviously they had nearly crossed the place. It was then that Lyn raised his head and sniffed the air. Ever since he had joined the first commando back in Scotland in '40, he had stopped smoking in the hope that it would improve his sense of smell. He had thought he ought to if he were going to become a good commando, though he had loved the comfort his old briar pipe had given him. Now he got a whiff of that almost forgotten odour immediately. It was Indian cooking: that mix of garlic, saffron, chillies and half a dozen herbs which was totally different from the rotten fish mix that the natives of the Malay peninsula used to spice their rice. He stopped short.

Jenkins raised his weapon, on the alert at once. 'Sir?' he whispered.

'There are Indians of some kind up there,' Lyn whispered back, and now the two of them could see the faint pink flickering of a fire to their right some way off. 'What are Indians doing in this godforsaken place?'

'Who knows what wogs do and why?' Jenkins said. He was a pre-war regular who had seen service on the North-West Frontier back in the thirties. 'Funny mob, Indians.'

Lyn wasn't listening. Now his mind raced as if he was considering the problem. There were no Indians, not even Tamils, in this part of the world. The only Indians were the ones who had surrendered with the rest of the British Army in '41/'42. So who was it out there cooking and what was he – Lyn supposed it would be a he – doing on this supposedly uninhabited island?

Lyn made his decision. They needed this island base; everything was predicated on its use as the point from which they'd attack Singapore. 'All right, Jenkins, let's have a look-see. No shooting if it's not absolutely necessary.'

'Sir.'

They moved forward, walking on the side of their feet, as they had been trained to, placing each foot down carefully, feeling first with the boot for any dry twig or the like that might snap and give their presence away. The smell of cooking grew stronger. They could hear voices too – the sing-song voices of Indians – but Lyn couldn't make out which of the scores of Indian languages the unknowns were speaking.

They edged ever closer. Lyn could hear his heart beating; it sounded very loud. Surely the Indians, whoever they were, could hear it. They didn't. Now and then they shouted like he remembered the sepoys doing back in the old days when they had had too much army-issue rum. He told himself that was good. They were celebrating. They'd be off their guard. Not all of them, however. In that same instant two dark figures in turbans walked purposefully across the track. They could make out the familiar outline of Lee-Enfield British Army rifles slung over their shoulders. They froze as one, hearts beating furiously.

For one moment the two commandos in the shadows thought they hadn't been seen. They were wrong. A sudden challenge. The click of a rifle bolt being drawn back. They had been spotted. Corporal Jenkins didn't wait for the challenge. He tucked the Sten gun against his hip. Next instant he opened fire. A scarlet flame stabbed the velvet darkness. There was the stink of burnt cordite. An instant later the leading Indian screamed high and hysterical like a woman.

Now Lyn didn't hesitate. He leapt forward, firing as he ran. A shadowy figure leapt out of the trees to his right. He caught the glint of pearly-white teeth. He dashed forward wielding his razor-sharp commando knife. Suddenly he was seized by the unreasoning bloodlust of combat. He smashed the brass knuckles of the knife into the man's face. He reeled back, but didn't go down. Lyn sprang upon him. Like a maniac, he slashed that murderous blade from left to right. The Indian went to his knees. His rifle fell from his shoulder. Savagely Lyn went in for the kill. 'Please . . . please . . .' the man pleaded in English. 'Mercy, for God's sake, sahib!'

But God was looking the other way this night and mercy had vanished from the earth. Lyn thrust his knife into the man's chest. He gasped. The knife slid ever deeper. Lyn knew all the tricks. He turned the blade with a quick movement of his wrist. Next moment he ripped it upwards, feeling the hot sticky blood flush his hand. The Indian might well have been dead already, transfixed by that terrible knife, held upright by it. Gasping furiously like a someone in the throes of a rapturous sexual orgasm, he kicked the man. His victim sighed, as if he were glad it was all over, and fell backwards slowly to lie dead on the blood-soaked lalang grass.

Now everything was confusion, hysterical chaos, as if the Indians felt they were being attacked by a herd of wild beasts – which they were, in a way. They fired wildly in every direction. They yelled. They shrieked. They cried contradictory orders and then Pongo and the Druid were beside Lyn and Jenkins, firing controlled, well-aimed bursts into the Indians' ranks.

Gasping for breath, his eyes wild and staring, Lyn raised his blood-dripping bayonet and cried above the crazy racket, 'Kill the lot of them . . . Don't let any of 'em escape, Pongo.'

Grimly Pongo raised his tommy gun again and, swinging from left to right like some gunslinger in a Hollywood movie, he mowed down the Indians to his immediate front. The Druid joined in. Reluctantly. He hadn't the same wild atavistic lust to kill that possessed the others. His pious Welsh chapel upbringing saw to that. Still, he took part in that crazy merciless slaughter with the rest, for he knew, as they did, that their lives depended upon not letting the Indians escape and perhaps report the presence of the commando on the island.

Here and there, the Indians tossed down their rifles, fell to the ground and cried as they tried desperately to escape that murderous fire by burrowing into the earth with their bare hands. *'No shoot . . . please . . . no shoot!'* But the shooting continued until, finally, as if waking from some terrible nightmare, Lyn ordered, in a voice that he hardly recognized as his own, 'Cease fire . . . cease fire, chaps!'

A loud echoing silence followed as they slumped there, bent and gasping, leathern-lunged like exhausted athletes after some great race. The silence seemed to go on for ever. Thus they stayed until they heard the metallic click of Corporal Jenkins reloading the magazine of his Sten. Still they didn't move, although they knew why Jenkins had reloaded. He was an old soldier. He knew what was to be done and he wanted to spare the CO from even giving the order to carry out what had to be done. They waited there numbly, still gasping harshly for breath, as they heard Jenkins tap the new magazine of his Sten to check whether it was firmly in place. It was. Jenkins stepped forward, taking a few paces to where the first of the Indian dead lay, slumped in heaps like bundles of abandoned rags. He touched the first one with the toe of his jungle boot, as if the body were indescribably dirty. The Druid's hands shot to his ears. He didn't want even to hear what happened next. But before Jenkins could fire the first of the shots that would blast the backs of the Indians' skulls off to ensure that they were really dead, there was a sudden burst of noise that made all of them jump. It was that of an outboard motor starting up.

Lyn moaned abruptly like a wild animal trapped and in pain. One of the Indians had escaped!

Book Five
Operation Malay Tiger

One

Lieutenant Kimura drew off his slippers, took off his gown so that he was now completely naked and drew back the sliding door to the *onsen*, the bathing house. Two girls were waiting for him. They were naked too. Although their bodies were still firm, with nice up-tilting breasts, they were older than he was. It didn't matter. That meant they were more experienced and they would get on with the business without too much fuss or the silly giggling of the younger girls of joy.

Although they were already in the warm water to their waists, they bowed very politely. He knew why. Like everyone else in Singapore, they were afraid of the Kemptai. He returned their bow with a slight one of his own. He didn't believe in showing too much respect to paid women, especially now when he was in love with the pure maidenly Iris, who couldn't possibly imagine what he intended to do in a few minutes.

He slipped into the water. It was indeed agreeably warm, but not warm enough to sap his desire.

The girls waited till he had slipped beneath the water up to his chest, then came across to him slowly, taking care not to splash. Naturally they didn't want to pollute his body with any water that might be dirtied from their own. He noted the action and approved. He believed in order and self-restraint. That was why he liked Iris. She, too, was very restrained. Even when by chance he came in contact with her slim body, she didn't react angrily as a well-born girl in Japan might have done. She simply moved away slightly without comment.

That was in a way his reason for attending the bathhouse in the officers' brothel. He would be seeing Iris later and by then he wanted his passion and desire to be muted so that she would have no occasion to take offence at him. The two whores would ensure that his sexual needs would be taken care of by then, and he could be free of desire for the single hour Iris's mother had apparently allowed her daughter to be with him after school.

The bigger of the two naked women bowed and said, 'With your permission, sir?'

He nodded and waited.

Cunningly her right hand slipped under the surface of the water. He felt a quickening of his heartbeat. He certainly needed sexual relief, he told himself. It had been a whole week since he had had a woman; he had been fully occupied trying to find more evidence to thoroughly convince that pig Tanaka of his theory that the English were going to attack Singapore harbour.

The whore brushed the side of his penis with her fingertips. He gasped, as if with pain. An electric shockwave of lust swept through his skinny frame. She grinned, noting the tumescence. Gingerly, as if it might be dangerous, she ran her fingers the length of his organ. She looked shocked and turned to the other whore, saying to her in an awed voice. 'It's huge!' She drew in her breath sharply.

Opposite, the other whore flung up her washcloth, the *tenegui*, into her face, as if she could not bear to look at such a monstrous erection.

The young lieutenant gave a tight grin. They were a good team. They played their roles well. He felt he would enjoy their attentions. He was right. The two of them were experts in giving men pleasure – for money. The older one kept tugging skilfully at his penis. But just when he felt he could contain himself no longer, she would release her grip and the intensity of his desire would diminish for a moment or two. Then she would start working on that tight pillar of engorged flesh once again.

In the meantime the other one had waded across lazily. Now she was directly behind him. She seized his hips in a tight grip. He liked the feeling, but wondered what she was up to. He soon learned. She thrust her pelvis against his skinny buttocks forcefully, with a deep bass grunt. It was as if she were a man making love to him from the rear. He gasped out loud, the sound choked and strangled. She laughed and did it again, saying, 'You like this, don't you, Lieutenant?'

He nodded numbly. He couldn't speak. He was so excited. He felt his loins might explode at any moment. God, how he liked it!

Abruptly the one stroking him so expertly and excitedly broke off. He opened his mouth to protest. But she backed away, spreading her legs as if she were swimming. He caught a glimpse of jet-black pubic hair as her legs opened wide and then she was clinging to the other side of the bath, her dark eyes challenging him. Her legs were still wide-open in invitation.

For a moment Lieutenant Kimura was at a loss. Was this part of the game? Or did she want to get it over with; did she want him to fuck her? Before he could decide, the cunning little bitch behind him grabbed him firmly by the hips once again, pressing her wet belly against his buttocks. Before he could catch on, she was propelling him forward, with his penis like the prow of an ancient

149

junk. He understood. She was going to push him into that hot quivering wet source of all delight.

He knew it was undignified to be directed like this by a woman. Women had to play the passive role. Even well-educated Christian women knew that. But he was too excited to protest. Even under the water, he could smell the hot rancid odour of a woman on heat. It wasn't just a game; the whore wanted him, too, he knew that implicitly.

He felt himself trembling with sexual delight. He could hardly focus his gaze on the woman's face as she looked at him almost tauntingly, her mouth slack and wet, her lips gleaming a bright red. He swallowed hard, trying to contain himself. He *had* to hold on. He couldn't let go yet. He felt the hand of the whore making him part his legs. What was she up to? Next moment he knew. She had grasped his penis from behind. She squeezed his testicles gently. It almost finished him there and then. Somehow he held on. Holding on to him by his genitals, she started to direct him into the other woman, mouthing obscenities into his right ear all the while. Holding on to the side of the bath, the other woman waited, licking her bright-red lips, as if in anticipation.

'Oh God!' he moaned, his sweat-lathered face contorted with almost unbearable sexual desire.

He felt the woman waiting, thrusting her loins forward to meet him. The tip of his erection nudged her stomach. It was like a soft silken pillow. His body seemed on fire. He couldn't wait any longer. No. He grabbed at her wet naked shoulders frantically, while behind him the other whore, still pushing forwards, laughed cynically. Unpleasant thoughts about the two of them shot through his tormented mind. They were making a tool, a male tool of him, to be used like this . . . But

what did it matter? He must have the woman now.
'I—'

He never completed the urgent demand. Behind him
the sliding door was nearly ripped from its flimsy frame.
There was the clatter of a sword on the wet tiles of the
bathhouse and a familiar and hated voice, heavy with
drink already, said, as if in triumph, 'Ah, so the good
Christian from Nagasaki also indulges in depravity, eh!'

The face of the woman before him suddenly twisted
into fear, all thoughts of sex abruptly vanished. His
erection withered in that same instant and behind him
the other whore let go of his hips as if they were red-hot.
Covering her breasts protectively, she splashed to where
her friend cowered, clutching her shoulders, so that they
looked now like two frightened children sheltering before
a tremendous storm.

Miserably, Lieutenant Kimura turned and faced Colonel
Tanaka framed in the doorway, face flushed with drink,
pig-like eyes seeming to pop out of their sockets. Behind
him towered a huge Indian with a turban, clad in the khaki
uniform of the Indian Legion, part of the Indian National
Liberation Army formed by the Japanese from their Indian
Army prisoners. He was trying to look away from the
whores, as if their nakedness was an embarrassment.

Tanaka wasted no more time. 'Well, Lieutenant, this is
a fine way to spend an afternoon. Have you no duties?'

Hurriedly Kimura pulled himself together. The best he
could, he gave a little bow. 'I have taken leave, sir . . . I
have an appointment later, sir.'

Tanaka grinned at his embarrassment. 'I can see you
have. Well, you have no appointment now. Get your
uniform on and come outside at once.'

'Immediately, sir.'

Tanaka swung round and nodded to the big Indian. The

man stepped aside to let the Kemptai officer swagger by, his fat buttocks trembling inside his breeches, his absurd sword clanking on the tiled floor. Kimura turned to the whores. They giggled, relieved that Tanaka had gone. Kimura felt himself flushing. 'I shall pay when I am dressed,' he snapped.

They giggled again. Then they bowed hastily. After all, Kimura was a member of the dreaded secret police too.

Five minutes later he was outside, still damp from the bath, blinking in the sudden bright sunlight. Tanaka and the big Indian officer in the turban were waiting for him. To either side of the street, the usual crowd of beggars, refugees and peddlers kept their distance, flowing around them like a river round a rock. All save a wretched half-naked coolie, cursing as he tried to pump up his flat tyre, which seemingly refused to be inflated. He saluted and Tanaka smiled at him cynically. 'Ay, the joys of the bathhouse!' he said, his pig-like little eyes red with drink.

Kimura said nothing and the big Indian, who obviously didn't speak Japanese, looked from one to the other in bewilderment.

But now Tanaka didn't waste time. 'It seems, Lieutenant, that despite your careless attitude to the service of our Imperial Majesty –' he drew his breath in sharply, as the usual sign of respect – 'you have hit the nail on the head. Now I have some reason to suspect that you are right. The English enemy is planning some sort of an attack on Singapore.' He turned to the Indian and said in slow awkward English, 'Captain Singh, will you please tell junior officer –' he indicated Kimura – 'what you know.'

The big Indian snapped to attention and saluted in the English fashion, though he was superior in rank to

Kimura. 'Sir, we are in training for raids against the English imperialists in Burma. Part of our training was to make little attacks on the outlying islands. One was set for the island of Merapas seventy miles from here.'

'When?'

'Three days ago. Twenty men with a boat took part. The details are obscure. But my men bumped into other armed men. One only escaped. He has been wounded and is not expected to live, but he has told me enough for me to conclude that my men bumped into an advance party of English.'

The Indian's command of English was excellent and he was a fast speaker. But Kimura – the whores and the delightful Iris forgotten now – kept up with him. It seemed he had been right all along. 'How do you know, Captain,' he asked in his best university English, 'that these men who fired on your fellows were English?'

The Sikh, who had been well trained by the English before he had turned traitor, opened the brass buckles of the haversack attached to his immaculate belt swiftly. He pulled out what looked like a piece of bloodstained green cloth. 'When my man was wounded and making his escape back to his boat, he picked this up to help staunch a wound in his side. You can see the blood—'

'Yes, yes,' Kimura said, cutting him off, hardly able to conceal his excitement now, while Tanaka looked on benevolently, as if he had arranged everything and was happy that his young charge was having this moment of triumph. 'Please – the English?'

The tall Indian unfolded the green cloth and now Kimura could see it was the kind of cap the English soldiers wore. Like such things, this was adorned with a tarnished badge. It seemed to depict the globe. The Indian kept him in suspense no longer. 'This, sir, is the badge of the English Royal Marines. Once these Marines were used by the English for their cruel imperialist adventures. Now the Marines are what are called the commandos. Green is their colour. And these commandos are used for raids on enemy territory.' He stopped as if he knew he had played his part and his new Japanese masters, the authors of the new Co-Prosperity Sphere to which he now proudly belonged, needed him no longer.

The two Japanese officers looked at each other significantly, as Kimura accepted the bloodstained green beret wordlessly from the Indian. Opposite, the coolie had stopped pumping, as if he had come to the conclusion that it was no good. The Raleigh and its threadbare pre-war tyres had had it; they were beyond repair. But, if anyone had taken any notice of him – though no one did, for he was just an ignorant coolie fated to die young – they would have noted a keen look of interest in his dark eyes as he stared as if hypnotized at the green cap.

Finally Tanaka broke the silence. 'Perhaps,' he said in his laboured English, 'we shall drink . . . and discuss this?' In Japanese he said to Kimura, 'Or have you another kind of appointment?' He made an obscene gesture, thrusting his forefinger back and forth rapidly into a circle of flesh formed by his thumb and second finger.

Kimura shook his head. 'No sir!' he snapped, very businesslike at this moment, even forgetting Iris.

But someone hadn't. Cursing and angry, the half-naked coolie with the Raleigh started to push it to where Iris would soon be waiting for him outside school.

Two

The next week was what Pongo O'Dare called 'a mixed bag' for Operation Malay Tiger. They all knew, even the dullest of them, that the operation might have been compromised by that lone escapee from the bunch of Indian Army traitors – as they felt them to be – whom they had massacred on Merapas. Lyn had no idea whether he had actually lived. They had found traces of his fresh blood on the beach and the Druid, as their medic, had opined that he'd been 'hit bad'. Still, he *had* had strength enough to escape – but to where, they did not know.

On the first day they had set up an ambush on the beach to slaughter anybody that the unknown escapee might have brought back to the island. But the flat, shimmering blue waste of the Java Sea had remained empty. Thus, after the next dawn stand-to, Colonel Lyn had allowed an issue of rum for all of them, save the Druid, who had declared roundly, 'I'll have no truck with the demon drink,' which had occasioned Blue to call out, 'Silly Welsh bugger, turning down grog! Yer never know, cobbers, when you'll get another.' How true that statement was, he'd find out soon enough.

After Corporal Jenkins had dished out half a mugful each from the big quartermaster's jug, Lyn had said, 'Well, chaps, perhaps the treacherous bugger didn't get away after all.' He had looked around at their tough

155

bronzed faces, dark shadows under their eyes from the lack of sleep over the last forty-eight hours. 'Anyway, I'm going to go ahead with the op. But I don't think this island ought to be our base for long. So, this is what I'm going to do. I'm going to leave our heavy stores here. Hide them deep in the jungle. They should be OK there for a few days. Then, apart from the stores guard, the rest of us will use the *Porpoise* – I've already signalled her skipper to come in closer at six hundred hours, just after dawn. What we'll do then is sail closer to Singapore and attempt to seize a civilian junk, something like that, to use for the actual attack on the base. I know this is all rough-and-ready and not our actual original intention, But that's the way things are in war. Things never go straight in – like the actress said to the bishop.'

That raised a tired laugh and, although the Druid frowned, he realized what his beloved CO was about. Since the unknown Indian had escaped in his boat an element of the unknown and danger had entered their mission. Another and lesser commander might well have scrubbed the whole operation in such a situation, but not Colonel Lyn. He had worked so hard, going right to the top to do so, in order to get Operation Malay Tiger approved. Now, if he could, he was going to see it through.

Two days later they found what Lyn was looking for. Cruising on the surface just before dawn off the coast of Borneo, the officers on the conning tower of the *Porpoise* spotted a two-masted junk on the horizon, proceeding at a leisurely pace. After Commander Marsham had taken the usual safety precautions, checking the sky carefully – for the junk might well have been the bait to lure them into the bombing sights of an enemy plane – they had come up close to the junk. They had surveyed it again very carefully. Her name was *Mustika* and, as far as they could ascertain from the dress of the native steersman, her crew were some sort of Indonesians. But, as Lyn said, 'Even if they are working for the Nips, I don't think they could cause my lads much trouble.'

It was a thought with which Pongo agreed in his usual hearty fashion, slamming a big fist into the palm of his other hand. 'Just let 'em try!' he snorted.

Lyn grinned and added, 'There's no sign of a radio mast either. So let's do it, chaps.'

The commandos didn't need a second invitation.

In five minutes they were swarming up the wooden sides of the junk, catching the dark-skinned crew in their turbans and long sarongs completely by surprise as they ate their breakfast rice, covered in a green, evil-smelling fish paste. But the Indonesians were friendly enough. They showed the commandos how to handle their craft, which was steered by a kind of long oar, and which navigated by what looked like a medieval lodestone instead of a compass. As Blue snorted, 'Strewth, it's like the Dark Ages – and I bet they don't have a pot to piss in either.' For once, the big Australian was right. The *Mustika*'s only sanitation was a kind of rough bamboo cradle attached to the stern, in which a man had to balance himself precariously and judge the waves if he were to evacuate his bowels successfully and not make a mess of himself.

But despite the primitive quality of the junk, Lyn was well satisfied with it. He didn't think the Japs would ever suspect there might be white troops aboard such a vessel. Hastily he made his new plan. The Sleeping Beauties, plus a couple of the folboats, were transferred to the junk and hidden under the spare sail. The commandos who were to sail with Lyn were ordered to strip to the waist and tie anything that looked like a sarong around their waists and pose as natives whenever they thought they might be observed.

It was an order that caused the Druid to be mercilessly ragged by the others, especially by Blue and his fellow Aussies. Time and time again they tried to flip up his 'skirt', as they called it, intoning in what they thought was a Scots accent, '*Chase me . . . Chase me, Charlie, for I'm the cock o' the North,*' until Pongo intervened, snapping, 'Make any more of that racket and *you*'ll be the cocks of the ruddy north. The Nips in Singapore'll probably be able to hear the racket you lot are making.'

That sobered them up a little, for even the thickest of the commandos knew now that they were venturing into the unknown and the hasty plans that Colonel Lyn was making with the skipper of the *Porpoise* would be filled with imponderables.

They were. Even Lyn had to admit as much to Marsham, as they sat in what shade from the fierce tropical sun was offered by the submarine's conning tower, scanning the charts of the Java Sea, working out timetables and rendezvous, knowing nothing more of the area than what they could learn from the Admiralty maps.

'The way I see it, Hubert,' Lyn told the Navy officer, 'the less time we spend in the junk the better. I don't think it would stand close scrutiny by some Jap patrol boat.'

Hubert Marsham nodded his agreement.

'So I have decided to head for Pompong Island here.' His forefinger stabbed the chart. 'I'll have to take a chance that it is inhabited, but it doesn't look big enough or important enough to be occupied by the Japs.'

'Agreed.'

'So, we'll use it as our forward base and perhaps *here* – Subar Island – which is even closer to Singapore harbour. The junk will be our means of transportation. I don't think we'll be at sea more than a couple of hours at a time.'

'Yes. And try to use darkness as much as possible,' Marsham suggested. Those wooden junks give off no radar echo, of course. So that will make the trip even safer during the hours of darkness.'

Then the two officers got down to questioning what they'd decided and the timing of the rendezvous with each other, once Operation Malay Tiger had been completed.

It proved difficult because Lyn couldn't give a definite date for the attack. In the end, with Marsham not prepared to risk his submarine for a long period in Japanese waters, they agreed that the *Porpoise* should return to base. In forty days' time, whether Lyn had carried out his mission or not, Marsham would rendezvous with him at a point and bearing to be decided in thirty days' time by radio.

With unusual ceremony, the two of them rose, the one still in the clean whites of a submarine commander in His Majesty's Royal Navy, the other half-naked, wearing a coolie's straw hat and with his upper body darkened even more by dye. Under other circumstances, they would have presented a strange picture as they solemnly and wordlessly shook hands. Not now. For there seemed something almost heroic in their parting. They faced each other for what seemed a long time, then the submarine commander said, 'Goodbye, Ivan.' He had experienced many such partings during this long war and yet he said the words with feeling, as if he were doing so for the very first time.

Later, as he and his second in command watched the *Mustika* slowly begin to pull away and, below, the crew prepared to dive, he said, 'Well, what do you think, Number One?'

His number one wasn't an impressionable man either;

submarine officers who risked their lives every time they went out on a fighting patrol couldn't afford to be. He answered straightaway, not querying what the skipper meant: 'Dodgy, sir . . . decidedly dodgy.'

'Me, too,' Marsham answered.

On the *Mustika*, Lyn waved farewell, and shouted something which Marsham couldn't quite make out.

He waved back. Then he turned. His head bent slightly, he clambered down the ladder into the green-glowing interior of the submarine. A moment later 'Jimmy the One' followed. His mood was equally sombre. He guessed, as he was sure the skipper had, that they'd never see Colonel Lyn and his men again.

Three

I t was three days later.
The secret invaders had reached the new base
at Pompong Island without incident. Twice low-flying
Japanese reconnaissance planes had buzzed the *Mustika*.
Both the disguised British and the Indonesian crew had
waved frantically and the enemy pilots had taken them for
friendlies and had flown away, leaving them in peace.

The island of Pompong had proved to be uninhabited.
Once there had been a native settlement there but it had
been abandoned a long time before. The huts had fallen
into disrepair and the weeds and jungle creepers had soon
covered the vanished natives' gardens. The only things
they had left behind had been a welcome addition to the
invaders' larders – domestic pigs which had escaped and
gone wild. That first night on Pompong they had enjoyed
a pig roast, native style, the carcasses roasted whole on
hot stones and covered with great fronds of palm leaves
to keep the meat succulent.

That night, satiated with the fresh meat and relaxed
after a tot of issue rum, the men had slept in the open,
ignoring the hum of the mosquitoes and the occasional
showers, pleased with the world and themselves. Even
Corporal Jenkins had relaxed, maintaining, 'This is real
peacetime-regular-army style. Life of frigging Riley!'

Despite the corporal's cuss word, even the Druid had

been forced to agree. Indeed, he was so relaxed that night that he almost forgot to say his nightly prayers until a large mosquito stung him and he felt the good Lord was reminding him of his duties.

Now, while those who were left on the island prepared defensive positions and worked on the explosives and the like to be used in the attack, Corporal Jenkins, the Druid and Pongo lay up on the island of Subar, which was so close to Singapore harbour that it was plainly visible through the telescope they had loaned from the *Porpoise*.

With Corporal Jenkins standing guard with his silenced Sten gun, the two others had clambered up a palm tree, camouflaged themselves with fronds up at its crown and had tied themselves in position with their toggle ropes. Surveying the harbour, they had sketched the best they could the various points and, more importantly, the positions of the shipping. Later, Pongo knew, they could compare their sketches with the silhouettes in *Jane's Fighting Ships* and identify the ones that were most important and made the best targets for their limited supply of limpet mines.

It was thus that Lyn found them when the *Mustika* sneaked into the island's little concealed bay. It was planned he would bring them out that evening and return to Pompong Island, where, with the help of their sketches, they would finalize the plan for the great attack.

Together the four of them enjoyed the fresh lime juice that the Indonesian crew had prepared for them and which they had kept quite cool by some means or other. Then, before the light went altogether, Lyn shinned up the tree himself and had a look at the scene. With the telescope he swept the harbour, making a mental comparison with the sketches his two lookouts had made that day. Suddenly he stopped short. To the left he could just make out the usual superstructure and masts of a large Japanese warship – it could be a heavy cruiser to judge by its size. It was coming down the Straits of Malacca and obviously heading into the harbour for the night. He whistled softly. A cruiser, what an achievement that would be if they could blow her up. So far, in nearly three years of war against Japan, the whole of the Royal Navy had not been able to sink a Jap ship of that size. Now, if a troop of commandos could do it . . . He didn't dare think the thought to its logical end.

So, it was with his mind buzzing, despite his tiredness after the long hot day, that Lyn began to make his plans as the little junk crept out of the bay and hugged the coast on its way back to Pompong Island.

Their progress was slow and, although it was darkening rapidly, they sailed without riding lights. It was dangerous, but Lyn reasoned they had to take the chance of bumping into some native fishing vessel. They didn't want any Japanese lookout posted along Sumatra's eastern coast to spot them. If a native craft did challenge them, he relied on the Indonesians to talk them out of any difficulties. They had been well bribed by what they called 'the Horsemen of St George', gold sovereigns featuring St George, the dragon-slayer, on his horse. Besides, he was too busy working out his new plan for attacking the Jap cruiser to worry too much about the chance of being discovered. They had dodged the enemy up to now, why should the present and future be any different?

But, unknown to Lyn, his luck had run out at last. It was when they were passing close by the island of Kasu an hour later that, to their surprise, they found themselves crossing a small bay which didn't seem to be marked on their charts. Along the coast he could see the flickering of coconut lights, with here and there the bright white light of petroleum lanterns. Lyn concluded that he was close to a sizeable coastal fishing village, something of that kind. But there was nothing he could do about it now. The wind was against the junk. Anyway, if anyone was watching them on the shore, they would only encourage suspicion if they changed course now. He looked glumly at Pongo, who had also realized their danger now, and said: 'Better put the lads on double watch, Pongo. You never know.'

'Immediately, sir,' Pongo responded hastily and, calling for Corporal Jenkins, he set about posting concealed lookouts, all heavily armed and prepared for anything

Now, due to the shape of the coast, they were edging ever closer to the nearest houses, crude log huts raised on wooden piles driven into the sand of the beach, surrounded by battered old fishing boats and what looked like nets strung out to dry or be repaired for the next morning's fishing. Crouched behind the native helmsman, revolver in hand, Lyn felt the tension beginning to mount and, despite the evening breeze, he was sweating once more. The hand holding his revolver was damp with perspiration. He told himself to get a grip on himself. It would take perhaps twenty to thirty minutes to clear the village and then they'd be around the cove and out of sight. Besides, why should the local fishermen be interested in one of their own junks? They probably saw them ten times a day.

But even as he attempted to reason with himself, his ears were making out the first asthmatic chug-chug of an ancient engine; and native fishermen didn't have craft with engines! A boat was moving somewhere among the shoreside huts on piles and coming their way. He raised himself slightly and, in a voice hoarse with renewed tension, called, 'Stand by everybody . . . I think there's a craft coming our way.' In front of him the native helmsman muttered something in his own language and, although Lyn couldn't understand the words, he guessed they signified that the Indonesian was scared too.

Moments later an ancient launch came out from between the huts. It was flying the Japanese flag and up front Corporal Jenkins muttered, 'Scrambled-egg flag, sir.'

Lyn nodded his understanding and, straining his eyes in the gloom, he made out four natives who were obviously Malays from their colour, but who were wearing Japanese uniform, complete with battered peaked ski-type cap. Slowly, carefully, he clicked off his safety.

The launch came closer and closer. It was slowing down, however. Obviously the four Malays in Jap uniform were suspicious. They were going to examine the *Mustika*. The junk heaved to. The helmsman shouted something to the four Malays, who were all armed. They shouted back and Lyn gathered from the inflection of their voices that they were not unduly suspicious. Perhaps, he thought, they were employed by the Japs as a kind of auxiliary water police to check native traffic – and probably take backhanders from those who were carrying contraband. He hoped so. He started to breathe more quietly and his nerves, which in these last few weeks behind enemy lines had become very tense, calmed down somewhat.

Then suddenly, startlingly, everything went wrong. Corporal Jenkins popped up from his hiding place on the prow. The Malays saw him at once. The tallest cried out. It was clear that they had recognized Jenkins as a European straight away. A light on the bow of their launch clicked on. A harsh beam of cold white light swept the deck of the junk. The helmsman panicked. He let go of the big tiller. The junk swung round in the current. Corporal Jenkins panicked – or perhaps he did what he thought was correct. He stood up and with a harsh grimace and fully outlined by the probing beam, fired a burst at the launch. At that range he simply couldn't miss. The closest Malay flung up his hands screaming; a pattern of blood-red buttonholes were suddenly stitched across his skinny uniformed chest. Next moment he slammed to the deck, dead before he hit it.

Now all hell was let loose and, even as he rose to join in the one-sided battle, Lyn knew, with a sinking feeling, that Operation Malay Tiger had been compromised, perhaps hopelessly so.

But there was no time for recriminations now. Together with Pongo, Lyn started firing aimed shots at the search-light, hoping to knock it out so that they could escape before the sound of their firing attracted other of the enemy who might be stationed in the fishing village. But Corporal Jenkins, carried away by the crazy, unreasoning bloodlust of combat, had poised himself on the prow and was firing swift bursts along the deck of the launch, ignoring the light and the danger to himself.

His boldness paid off. Another Malay was hit. He crumpled slowly to the deck his guts welling up from his shattered stomach like a steaming ugly snake. The man next to him was hit too. He went down without a sound. That was it as far as the fourth Malay was concerned. Hastily he threw away his revolver. A moment later he had flung himself over the side of the launch and in blind panic was swimming with all his strength for the fishing village, which was already loud with shouts, barking dogs, screaming children. Behind him the light still blazed and the launch's motor ticked away like the beat of a metallic heart.

'Cease fire! . . . Cease fire!' Lyn yelled almost angrily, as the men continued to fire at the swimming man. 'Save your ammo . . .' His voice trailed away to nothing, but at the back of his head a cynical voice rasped, '*Because it looks as if you're bloody well gonna need it . . .*'

For a moment or two in the loud silence that followed the gun battle, Lyn didn't know what to do. All his energy, his powers of decision, the need to give immediate orders had vanished. He felt like a zombie drained of all willpower. It took his old friend Pongo to make him wake up to the urgency of the new situation. 'Sir.' Pongo's voice seemed to come from a long way off. 'What's the drill?'

Lyn shook his head like an exhausted man trying to wake up from a heavy dream. 'What?'

Pongo repeated his question.

Lyn was awake again. 'The drill? Why, Pongo, the drill is – *we run for our bloody lives!*'

Four

Lieutenant Kimura was elated. His keen young face shone with excitement, as yet another report of a sighting came in. He could have patted the cheek of the young naval signaller who had presented the signal to him. Instead he said, 'Thank you, very much, Murakami. Keep up the good work.' The signaller flushed with pleasure. It was very rare that officers spoke to humble second class sailors in that manner. He bowed, did a perfect about-turn and marched out stiffly as if he were parading before His Imperial Majesty, Emperor Hirohito, personally.

Kimura flashed another look at the brief message from Naval HQ, Singapore. 'White junk,' he read, 'reported off area Khota Baru. Air Reconnaissance alerted.' He told himself it had to be the Europeans reported by the Malay water policeman. White junks were uncommon in those waters; most of them were coloured a dull brown. the junk sighted by the surviving Malay policeman in Japanese service had also been white.

He strode over to the map on the wall and with his finger traced a route from Singapore to Khota Baru. He nodded and, in the manner of lonely men, said to himself, 'It fits in. Either they are attempting to flee or they are covering their tracks intending to double back and attack Singapore.' He frowned suddenly. But what hope had the English of attacking Singapore now that their craft, the

168

white junk, had been spotted? The English must know that every Japanese post and soldier would be on the lookout for them.'

He heard the heavy-booted stomp and the rattle of the trailing, overlong samurai sword in the corridor outside, which indicated that his chief, Colonel Tanaka, was approaching. He stepped back from the map hurriedly. 'Fronting the map', as he always put it, was the perk of senior officers, such as that fool Tanaka.

Next moment Tanaka flung the door open and appeared, red-eyed and flushed. He had obviously been drinking his lunch at the Senior Officers' Club yet again. Kimura clicked to attention and bowed. Vaguely Tanaka touched his right hand to the peak of his cap and, staggering a little, wound his way to his chair. He slumped into it, cap still on his shaven gleaming head, and said thickly, 'Get me a whisky from the cupboard!' He didn't say 'Please'; he never did. Scratch off the veneer of military rank, Kimura told himself angrily at being spoken to in this manner, and you'd find a damned ragged-arse peasant beneath.

Still, he poured the colonel a drink and brought it to him. Tanaka didn't say thank you. Instead, he drank a great gulp of the strong spirit and said, 'You look very pleased with yourself, Lieutenant.' He looked at the younger officer, a quizzical, mocking light in his pig-like eyes.

'With your permission, sir. I think I – we – have good reason to be pleased. Our theories about these English terrorists have been proved right. We know from all the reports that they are on the run and no longer in contact with their home bases.' He forced what he hoped was a warm smile, though his thoughts were not in the least warm as far as the fat drunken sot was concerned. 'And it can only be a matter of days before we apprehend them.

Then we can show to these fellow members of Japan's Co-Prosperity Sphere how the English Imperialists are prepared to destroy anything – even the shipping which brings them food – in their blind rage at our great victory in the East.' He smiled with genuine pride at Japan's military achievements.

Tanaka snorted. 'Idle dogs. They'll have to learn how to work like we Japanese do before they can share in our prosperity. But no matter, the dogs have their uses, eh?'

Kimura didn't know exactly what the colonel meant, but all the same he didn't hesitate to bow slightly and agree. 'Undoubtedly you are very right, Colonel.'

'Of course I am . . . I'm a colonel. Colonels are always right.' He chuckled and drained the rest of his drink. 'Naturally, generals are even more right. It goes with the rank. Well, you have done well, and you have helped me with my promotion.' He saw the look of interest in his subordinate's eyes and held up his fat paw swiftly to stop him asking what promotion. Instead he said, 'Naturally in my new position I shall need to improve my English. I can't command correctly if I can't give my orders properly. So I have decided to take a teacher to improve my knowledge of that bastard language, English.'

'Sir?' Kimura was completely puzzled at the way the conversation was going. His mind was full of the English saboteurs, whom he was so close to apprehending. Here, however, was the pig Tanaka babbling on in his drunken fashion about learning more English and the fact that he had taken on a teacher. Of what importance was that to the coming victory for Imperial Japan? Tanaka was now, however, to enlighten him.

He slammed the heel of his highly polished jackboot down on the desk in front of him so that his glass rattled and threatened to fall off. At the same time, he bellowed in his coarse parade-ground voice, 'Bring her in, Sergeant! At the double, now!'

'*Her*?' Kimura's mind started to query, but not for long. The door opened almost immediately and there, guided by one of the big Kemptai torturers, so that she looked even more the delicate petite girl child, was Iris.

Kimura gasped. He felt faint abruptly. His legs seemed about to fold beneath him, as his brain raced electrically, shocked out of all proportion by the sight of Iris in this place. He pulled himself together just in time and bowed slightly as Tanaka waved a hand in her direction and said proudly, 'My new English teacher, Miss Iris.' He said the title in English. 'I think you know her, Lieutenant Kimura?'

Kimura stammered something, he didn't know what. He was too shocked and bewildered. He stared at her, mouth open, gawping like some stupid peasant. She returned his look, no expression on her beautiful face, and then she turned attentively to the ogre, Tanaka, bowed and smiled and said in accented Japanese, 'It will be a great pleasure, sir, to work for you. Please, you must give me instructions.'

Tanaka licked his fat lips until they glistened a bright, wet blood-red. 'Don't worry, my little miss. I shall instruct you in your duties.' He shot Kimura a knowing look and said, 'But please don't let me detain you, Lieutenant. You must get about your duties. I want to tell Miss Iris what I want of her.' He drew the words out so that Kimura was quite clear what he intended.

For a moment he felt the rage well up inside him. He balled his fists and would have struck Tanaka there and then. But reason reasserted itself, though he knew that he would kill Colonel Tanaka, and damn the consequences, if he laid even a finger on Iris. But why had she agreed to do this? There was no answer forthcoming at that moment. He bowed therefore and went out, his heart full of hatred, hearing, as he marched out, Tanaka saying in a silky tone he had never heard from the pig before, 'Just because I'm a general now, my dear, you must not be afraid of me. Treat me like you would any other pupil. I'm just a quite harmless old man in reality . . . Now, may I offer you something to drink?'

As the door closed behind them, the big sergeant winked and murmured, 'The old man's got himself a fine young peach to be plucked there all right, hasn't he, sir?' And he winked knowingly once more.

It didn't take Kimura long to find out what had happened. Tanaka had been given command of one of the four Indian divisions of the Indian National Liberation, Army formed from ex-Indian Army POWs soon to be sent to Burma to fight against their former comrades. Due to the manifold dialects spoken by the Indian renegades, English was the lingua franca spoken in their divisions. Hence Tanaka's urgent need of an English teacher.

Swiftly the young officer, burning with rage and injured pride, had discovered that Tanaka had spoken personally with the principal nun of the college Iris had attended and had been directed by her to Iris's Japanese mother, who had apparently agreed to this innocent girl, with no teaching experience, being sent as the degenerate old officer's teacher of English.

Kimura could naturally understand the fear that Kemptai officers usually created among the local civilians, but why had Iris agreed to do this unusual job, leaving school to do so? No one in higher authority would have forced her to obey Tanaka's command; it would he seen in Tokyo as an abuse of the local population, more especially as Iris was half-Japanese. So *why?*

But that evening while he was still fuming, drinking heavily in the confines of his own quarters, mind racing frighteningly as he visualized what the cruel pervert might be doing to Iris at this very moment, news came in that penetrated even his drink-sodden brain and made him realize he must forget Iris for the time being and concentrate on the English saboteurs.

Four of the saboteurs had been trapped by an Imperial Army patrol on Pulo Sambol only twenty kilometres from Singapore itself. The English had driven off the Japanese patrol and now reinforcements, armed with a heavy machine gun, were on their way. They had been ordered by Army Command to wipe out the English.

Using the authority of Kemptai, which impressed even high-ranking regular-army staff officers, Kimura ordered that the English should not be killed. They had to be captured and brought to Singapore headquarters immediately for questioning. For he reasoned from what the Indian soldier and the surviving Malay policeman had related that there were more than four English commandos out there; and such bold men, who had come so far to carry out their daring mission, would not flee without making some attempt at sabotage. Kimura told himself he needed to know where the rest of them were.

Then he went back to his saki and his worries about the fate of Iris, who was confined with her pupil somewhere in this very same building. More than once he took his pistol out of its holster and slipped off the Mauser's safety catch. Should he deal with Tanaka once and for all, he moaned to himself as he slumped there looking down at the heavy weapon? But each time, drunk as he was, he told himself that would not be the solution. Assassinate Colonel – soon to be General – Tanaka and his fate would be sealed. He would be executed immediately so that the scandal could be hushed up. His murder would soon be followed by that of Iris. He knew the ruling military clique in Tokyo would clear the deck of all witnesses in order that the honour of the Imperial Army should be maintained. In the end, he gave up. He collapsed on his bed, drunk to the world, and fell into a heavy sleep, still moaning, 'Oh God, what shall I do?'

But the lovesick and very drunk young officer need not have worried. Others that night were preparing to take care of the newly promoted General Tanaka once and for all time. As Kimura snored harshly on his rumpled bed, the floor littered with empty saki bottles, the coolie on the battered Raleigh prepared to act at last . . .

Five

'Jenkins is still giving 'em stick,' Pongo said through gritted teeth as he helped push the second Sleeping Beauty into the water. He nodded his head in the direction that the steady hammer of a Bren gun was coming from. Tracer, red and white, zipped back and forth across the night sky in a lethal morse, interrupted by the obscene whack of a small Japanese mortar.

Lyn gave a final shove and the long craft slid into the water. To left and right, the other survivors grunted and shoved, straining every muscle to get their craft through the wet sand of the beach and into the foaming white surf. He relaxed for a moment and said a little sadly, 'Jenkins is a brave soldier, Pongo. If we ever get out of this mess, I'll recommend him for a gong.'

Ever cheerful, Pongo said, wiping the sweat off his brow, 'We'll survive, Ivan. We've been in tight spots before and got out of them. I know it's going to be shit or bust. But . . .' He shrugged and left the rest of his sentence unsaid.

They had sunk the junk and sent the crew off to find their own salvation. Then they'd headed for Pulo Sambol with their boats and as much gear as they could carry. But once again their luck had run out, as it had all too often in these last weeks. They had barely gotten ashore and commenced camouflaging the boats when they had bumped into the Jap patrol. Jenkins, who had been in charge of the advance party, had soon put the enemy to flight. But now he was bogged down fighting a much larger patrol and a very worried Lyn knew it could only be a matter of time before the Japs swamped his position – on a rise held by a handful of men – and rushed his own main party. In essence, Corporal Jenkins and his chaps were sacrificing themselves for the sake of the rest.

Pongo must have been able to read the CO's thoughts, for he asked, as the commandos launched another Sleeping Beauty, 'Shall we signal Jenkins to pull back, Ivan?'

Lyn pulled a face. 'I wish you hadn't asked that, Pongo.' He shook his head. 'I don't think so—' His words were drowned by the shriek of a mortar bomb falling out of the sky nearby and exploding in a shower of shingle up at the head of the beach. Red-hot shrapnel sliced through the air frighteningly. A trooper yelped with pain and clasped his hand to his right shoulder.

Blood started to seep through his tightly clasped fingers. The Druid rushed to help him. He waved the Welsh medic away, snarling, 'Bugger off, Taffy . . . Got to get them boats into the water.' He staggered off to help the others.

Lyn and Pongo did the same. They knew now that the Japs had outflanked Jenkins. His men were still firing, but now the Japs were going to concentrate on the larger party attempting to escape from the beach. The mortar was just finding its range. Once the enemy had got the range right, they would come charging in under the cover of the mortar fire. As Lyn and Pongo strained to get the third boat across the sand and into the surf, the former said, 'Get ready with your grenades, Pongo. In case . . .'

Pongo nodded and with a grunt, heaved his massive shoulder against the Sleeping Beauty, as if he were in an Army scrum back at pre-war Twickenham. Behind them the mortar howled yet again and another bomb came hurtling down furiously from the dark sky.

It was nearly five minutes later that the chatter of Jenkins' Bren gun erupted into a series of short stutters and then finally fell silent altogether. For a moment Lyn, straining desperately, the veins standing out at his temple with the effort, prayed that Jenkins had merely had a stoppage and that he'd begin firing again in a second.

That wasn't to be. Suddenly there was a last burst of rifle fire followed a moment later by a series of blood-curdling shrieks and someone screaming in English, 'Please . . . please . . . not that!'

'Frigging hell!' Blue cried. 'They're slaughtering the poor sods!'

Lyn knew the big Aussie was right. But there was no time to honour Jenkins and his men's sacrifice now. The Japs would be coming in a minute. 'Pongo, take the main body and get into the boats.'

Another bomb exploded nearby. In its blood-red glare, Lyn could see Pongo opening his mouth to protest. He didn't give him a chance to do so. 'That's an order! At the double!'

'Blue, get a half dozen blokes and follow me!'

'Sir.'

In the same instant that the rearguard under Lyn reached the head of the little beach, the Japanese burst out of the mangroves, led by a diminutive officer whirling his sabre and crying, '*Banzai*! *Banzai*!' He sounded as if he were drunk or drugged, perhaps both.

'Strewth!' Blue cried. 'I'll fuckin' banzai yer, mate!' He fired his tommy gun straight from the hip without appearing to aim. The officer screamed. The whole front of his upper body disappeared in a welter of red gore.

The sword fell from his suddenly nerveless fingers. He dropped to the sand without a sound. For a moment the attackers faltered . . . but only for a moment. A burly sergeant to the rear yelled. The attackers surged forward once more. Straight into the concentrated fire of the rearguard.

The Japanese stopped as if they had run abruptly into an invisible wall. For what seemed an eternity, they twisted, they danced, they jigged back and forth like a bunch of puppets at the hands of a puppet-master who had suddenly gone crazy. Then they were falling everywhere – screaming, shrieking, crying for their mothers – finally to lie in throbbing quivering heaps.

Lyn acted quickly. 'Start pulling back. *Now!*' he yelled, his voice sounding far too loud in that sudden awesome silence of death. The men needed no urging. They backed off, gaze still fixed on the bushes and the mangroves beyond the heaps of Japanese dead. Fór they knew instinctively there were more of the enemy there, trying to summon up enough courage to make another charge. They had only minutes to get to the waiting boats.

Following the ragged line, a grenade in his left hand, Lyn fired carefully aimed shots from his revolver from one side of the little front to the other. He was hoping to keep the Japs pinned down till they reached the edge of the beach. But that first obscene belch of the hidden mortar and the howl of the bomb streaking into the night sky told him he wasn't going to manage it. Then, in the same instant that the mortar salvo came hurtling down with a banshee-like shriek, a flare burst directly above the little line of defenders. It outlined them the next moment in its icy silver light, making their every detail visible to the Japs.

'*Banzai!*' The battle cry split the silence. The Japanese

came rushing out of the bushes with their fixed bayonets, as if, with all their fanatical bravery, they couldn't die quickly enough.

'Fuck this for a game of soldiers!' Blue yelled and pulled the pin out of his grenade in the same instant that the volley slammed into his chest. He fell at the same moment that the grenade fell out of his abruptly nerveless fingers. He screamed shrilly like a woman in hysterics as the grenade flung him into the air in a frenzied blast of vivid red flame. Pieces of the dead Australian flew to all sides.

His violent death seemed to encourage the attackers. As man after man threw his single grenade, they renewed their charge, screaming that terrible *banzai* of theirs. Men fell everywhere. They closed with the retreating commandos. It became a battle between individuals. Entrenching tools, bayonets, knives sliced and flashed in that cold silver light. Men went mad. Heads were cleaved. Blood spluttered everywhere. Commando and Japanese rolled back and forth in the wet sand and shingle, gouging, biting, scratching, tearing. They were like wild animals trying to tear the life from each other with their bare claws.

A tall Japanese rushed Lyn with his bayonet. Lyn pressed his trigger. A flat click. He had run out of ammo! He flung the empty pistol at the triumphant Jap. It missed. The Jap roared. He lunged. Lyn dodged a little too late. He felt a red-hot burning pain sear his left arm. Instinctively he launched a kick at his attacker. It caught the Japanese a cruel blow in the crotch. He gave a great shocked gasp, staggered back, his bayonet lowered. Lyn didn't give him a chance to recover. He kicked him again and then whipped out his commando knife. He thrust it into the Jap's stomach, tugged him close to his own body and ripped the knife upwards cruelly. The Japanese soldier

179

gave a shriek. Lyn's hand was suddenly wet with hot blood. For a moment they clung together like two lovers in the throes of some unbearable passion. The Japanese's spine stiffened momentarily like a taut bowstring, then went slack. He gave one last gasp. He sagged in Lyn's arms. The officer gave a horrified shudder and pushed the Japanese away from him. He fell dead to the ground and then Lyn was pelting down to the waiting boats with the survivors while the others gave them covering fire.

Gasping and panting like asthmatics in the throes of some fatal attack, they threw themselves into the boats. Immediately their crews started to draw them away from that beach of death. A flare exploded above them. Again the fugitives were bathed in the cold merciless silver light. A Jap machine gun opened up. The tracer whizzed towards them. They crouched low in the Sleeping Beauties and folboats. The bullets zipped above their heads, twitching and tugging as they fell harmlessly into the water in tiny white eruptions of foam.

The mortar was different. Hastily the crew had run to the very edge of the beach and set up its tripod. In a flash they had the barrel attached, the sights raised and were shoving bombs into the tube like crazed automatons. The bombs began to fall out of the sky once more. 'Spread out,' Lyn cried desperately above the crazy racket. '*Spread out for Chrissake!*'

Now the bombs started to take their toll. It seemed that suddenly there were desperate men bobbing up and down in the water everywhere, yelling for help frantically, trying to keep themselves afloat, fighting to shed their heavy equipment before it was too late. But the merciless Jap fire was taking its toll. Now there were dead commandos in the shallow water, curled up in tight balls with the exquisite agony of their death, or floating flat on their faces like logs, being washed back and forth by the waves. Others had their hands clasped to their ears, frozen thus, as if in the moment of their death they had tried to cut out the noise of those bombs which meant their end.

'Swing them round!' Lyn called frantically, as some of the crews started to panic and fail to keep their craft prow-on to the waves. 'For God's sake, remember your drill!' Bile threatened to choke him, as he surveyed the terrible sight of his men being slaughtered without mercy. But he forced himself to ignore the dead and the dying and their piteous litany of pleas for help. It was the living who counted now.

Urgently he forced his own craft forward, aided by the Druid. A commando swam towards them. In the harsh cruel light of another flare, the Druid saw his crazed face and the blood-red foam oozing from his mouth and nostrils. 'Don't leave me, mates!' he pleaded piteously. 'Please don't leave . . . I've got a wife and kids back in blighty.' He reached out a hand, the bone glistening like polished ivory in the gory red mess of what was left of it.

'Don't let him aboard!' Lyn commanded. 'He'll capsize us. Get rid of him.'

'Sir—'

Lyn cut off the Welshman's plea brutally. 'You heard me . . . Get rid of him.'

'God bless you, Colonel,' the man with the shattered hand began. His words ended in a howl of absolute agony as the Druid struck at his hand with the paddle. He went under spluttering, the water above staining an immediate red. He came up again. Once more the Druid hit him, his face contorted with absolute horror at his own savage behaviour.

This time the commando didn't reappear. He went

under for good and the Druid collapsed, sobbing uncontrollably . . .

An hour later they were out of sight of land, four Sleeping Beauties and two folboats, perhaps with some twelve or fourteen men in all. Sombrely, silently, the men formed up in a circle around Lyn's and the Druid's Sleeping Beauty, tying their craft to each other with the toggle ropes. They were all exhausted, even Pongo, the giant. But it was not just their exhaustion that made them so silent; it was the remembrance of what they had just been through and the knowledge that so many of their comrades had been lost on that bloody shore. They were not even afraid. It was as if the future didn't concern them, and if it did, they knew *their* future would be short-lived and brutal and would end in fresh violence.

Lyn, who was trying to maintain tight water discipline, said, 'Open your water bottles and have a good drink, chaps. You deserve it.'

Without comment they did so, heads tilted back, taking great gulps of the tepid water, as if they were young recruits back in some country pub enjoying a pint after a tiring route march about which they would soon begin to boast. But now there would be no boasting, Lyn knew that. There would be little more marching for these survivors; they had almost reached the end of their march through life. He watched them and felt for them, sorry in a way that he had landed them in this mess. Yet at the same time he was proud of them and proud of himself. In war some had to die to ensure the survival of the others and to ensure their victory. This was what was happening now.

He waited till they had drunk their fill. Then he spoke, his voice low and a little weary, but with a resigned note in it. It was as if all the grand words had been said. Now the time had come for them to carry out their final duty and there could be no discussion about what that was going to be. 'Comrades, we are some fifteen kilometres or so away from Singapore. We can reach the outer anchorage by about one hundred hours tomorrow morning. We have one or two limpet mines per boat. I think we can do some damage with them still.' He paused. 'We shall rest here for half an hour and then we shall . . .' He didn't finish; he didn't need to. Obediently the survivors bent their heads over the paddles like men condemned and attempted to sleep. There was nothing more to be said . . .

Six

It was still cool. But the water-coolies were already out, sprinkling the length of the street on which the parade would take place. They padded back and forth to the water carts in front of the lines of excited Indian children who had been handed both an Indian and a Japanese paper flag and had already been told by the tall stern Sikh policemen, who were everywhere, how and when to wave them. Behind them the elders – it seemed the whole of Singapore's Indian community had turned out in force – waited stolidly underneath their white sun umbrellas. Only the Jewish community, the power behind the island city's economy, were talkative and noisy, but, as many Indians whispered to each other, 'Jews are always noisy.'

On the podium from which the great man and the celebrities would take the salute, junior Japanese staff officers, all gleaming boots and glistening gold staff lanyards, supervised the coolies, as they arranged the padded chairs, the microphones and the spitoons for the Indians. They did everything with typical precision, only raising their voices angrily when one of the coolies did something particularly stupid. Perhaps they knew it was a waste of energy to shout or even slap the half-naked scum. Coolies always made the same mistake again. Once they rounded on a coolie standing apparently idle near a rusty old bicycle. To the officers' surprise, he answered them in

184

their own language, telling them he had nothing to do with the work on the podium; he was just another spectator.

They were caught off guard and Lieutenant Kimura of the feared Kemptai was about to be summoned to quiz this strange coolie who could speak Japanese, when the detachment of the Imperial Guard arrived and, as usual, caused a minor sensation. For most of the non-Japanese present had never seen such tall Japanese soldiers before. In the excitement, the coolie pushed his bicycle away swiftly, wisely disappearing into the throng of Indian spectators.

The immensely tall men of the Imperial Guard goose-stepped to both sides of the podium. At the command of their officers, they went through the usual elaborate drill, the powder rising in little white clouds from their gloves as they slapped the butts of their rifles with immaculate precision before standing at ease to await the arrival of the Indian Division and its commanders.

Kimura frowned and looked at his watch yet again. Iris had arrived at General Tanaka's headquarters over half an hour ago. Why was it taking her so long to check the few words of English that General Tanaka would use in the coming ceremony? All he needed to say, Kimura knew, was, 'I salute you, *Netaji*. I promise you I will lead your brave Indian soldiers to victory.' That was all. His frown deepened. He knew what the decadent swine was up to. Now he wanted to take Iris to the front in Burma where his division of Indians would be thrown into the battle against the English. Instinctively Kimura's hand slipped down to his pistol holster. What kind of place was that for a delicate virginal girl like Iris? Hardly knowing that he was doing so, his mind full of dark suspicions and forebodings, he undid his holster flap and eased the pistol butt free.

For now he could hear the brassy blare of the Japanese

Army band coming from the city centre and, along the route, the giant Guards and their Sikh police auxiliaries were snapping to attention. The new division 'Free India' was on its way for the great farewell parade. Soon their '*Netaji*,' Dr Bose, would be appearing to address them – the Indian politician was invariably late.

Some two miles away in the outer reaches of Singapore harbour, Lyn and his survivors, ragged, exhausted and damp with perspiration, were still slipping from ship to ship attaching their deadly limpet mines. More than once they had thought they had been discovered. An hour earlier a sailor had actually leaned over the bulwark of his ship and they had frozen with shock directly below. They had been spotted! But the sailor had not seen them. He was too busy emptying a bucket of slops over the side and, instead of bullets, they had been at the receiving end of a mixture of foul rice and rotting vegetables.

Now, however, they had almost placed all their charges and Lyn was already planning an escape route, for he knew that their luck wouldn't hold much longer. The city was already waking up – in fact, he could hear the faint blare of a military band coming from somewhere. It wouldn't be long before the cruiser, which was to be their last target, started the usual routine of naval training exercises common to all navies when in harbour. Then her deck would be crowded with barefoot matelots going about their chores and duties. They'd spot the lone craft soon enough.

Followed by Pongo, he and the Druid pushed off from the hull of the merchantman they had just mined and, creeping along at three knots below the surface, steered towards the ugly silhouette of the enemy heavy cruiser. Slowly, very slowly, the Sleeping Beauty making virtually no sound, with hardly a ripple of white water to betray her presence in the midst of the enemy fleet, Lyn and the Druid edged their way around the camouflaged hull of the cruiser. It seemed to go on for ever, a giant steel cliff, with far too many openings out of which a startled head might pop at any moment and discover them there. But Pongo was keeping close up behind them and he had a silenced Sten gun in his hands now, ready to deal with the first stupid Jap who sounded the alarm. He, like Lyn, was going to sink that Jap cruiser, come what may. Like Lyn, Pongo too had fought the establishment for what seemed years to allow raiding forces such as this. A successful conclusion to Operation Malay Tiger would ensure that, whatever happened to them, the raiding parties with all their various kinds of X-Craft would continue their bold operations until the war ended in Allied victory.

Lyn switched off the engine. He had found the spot where he thought his limpet would have the best chance of sinking the Jap cruiser. Now, absolutely noiselessly, the Sleeping Beauty drew level with the spot. Operation Malay Tiger had commenced its last phase . . .

Solemnly the *Netaji*, dressed in a poorly fitting khaki uniform, complete with the same side-hat as his troops wore, filed up the steps of the podium to the cheers of the flag-waving Indian kids and the handful of Jews, who, for some reason, were wearing Indian-style turbans this morning. Below, the Imperial Guard stood to attention, while the band played traditional Japanese marching songs.

Burning with rage, Kimura watched as a smiling Tanaka, accompanied by Iris, swaggered up the steps behind the pudgy, bespectacled Indian leader. The fat pig seemed so full of himself, gallantly holding Iris's arm as she climbed up with him, as if he were some damned western gentleman of the old school. Kimura tried to calm himself, but everything seemed to make him angry this beautiful September morning, even the *Netaji*. Naturally in his line of work, he knew a lot about Bose. He had betrayed the Germans and the Indian volunteers for the *Wehrmacht*, just as he had done the British Indian authorities, suborning simple sepoys to join the Japanese Army; they now faced a British firing squad if they were ever captured by the enemy.

He watched as Bose prepared to speak with all the little vanities and gestures of the professional politician, pretending to consult notes, adjusting his big tortoiseshell glasses, tapping the microphone and the like. Kimura sniffed. The man had no real backbone, he told himself. Intelligence knew he was already sending secret couriers to Stalin, the Russian dictator. Thus, if Japan started to face defeat, Bose would be able to flee to Soviet Russia. Bose would do anything to achieve his aim – to become the dictator of his homeland. Once the *Netaji* had power in his fat, soft hands, Indian freedom would go out of the window.

The band stopped abruptly. The *Netaji* was about to speak. Tanaka drew himself up to his full height. Once the Indian puppet leader had finished spouting his rubbish, his division would march on to the parade ground, he would present it to the Indian and then the men would march off to the railway station, where the troop trains would be waiting for them. Thereafter, for two long days, he and the girl would be alone in the railway carriage suite which had been reserved for him as divisional commander. He licked suddenly dry lips at the thought. In two days anything could happen. There would be splendid first-class evening meals with French wine. Then at last he could relax, and who knew what the effect of that and her beautiful nubile virginal body might have on him. Perhaps the whores he had frequented, with their hard manner and cynical smiles when he had failed to perform yet again, had increased his problem? What he needed was a simple young girl, who he could *seduce*. Didn't the old saying have it right when it stated, 'appetite comes with the eating'? A long lazy seduction in the seclusion of that carriage might just do the trick. He smiled warmly at the thought of Iris naked and he, blessed at last with a massive erection, penetrating her, making her wriggle with sexual delight, gasping at the impact of that magnificent rod of hard, pulsating flesh. 'What joy!' he sighed. What indescribable joy!

At the microphone, Bose had begun to speak. 'Welcome to our brothers in arms,' he said in his few words of Japanese. 'We are greatly indebted to our allies of Great Nippon for this opportunity.' Then he lapsed into English, snarling, 'We of Free India will now do our duty. It may be that the British oppressors achieve some initial victories. But let me assure you –' he raised his right forefinger in the orator's traditional gesture of admonition – 'Great Britain has lost this war whatever happens. The only Allied victor will possibly be the United States . . .'

Tanaka frowned as the girl translated that bit. But he dismissed the matter almost immediately. What did politicians know about war? They never fought battles. Invariably they died of old age warm and snug in their own beds.

'But whatever happens, whether the Axis powers win or lose this war, the British oppressors will be thrown out of India. Now our soldiers, with the help of their Japanese brothers-in-arms, are prepared to go to battle to help speed up that glorious day! He raised his pudgy hand to his side-hat in a mockery of a salute. 'Comrades of all races, I salute you.' Then he flung both arms high into the air in the Japanese fashion, revealing the dark sweat patterns in the armpits. '*Banzai . . . Banzai . . .* !'

Immediately the band struck up. Tanaka snapped to attention. His division was coming up the street. Six abreast, their packs on their backs, rifles slung over their shoulders, the 'volunteers' from the Japanese POW camps swung into sight. Immediately the children began to wave their flags excitedly. Their elders clapped and even the Jews in their strange turbans seemed to be interested, though they neither cheered nor waved flags. They didn't have to. They knew the Japanese and the Indian merchants needed them to keep Singapore's economy going. They could almost do what they liked.

Proudly, their young brown faces lathered with sweat, the Indians marched towards the podium. Up front a *Jemadar* barked a command. The first company broke into the Japanese goose step. The men were unaccustomed to the step, but they did their best. Bose beamed. His chaps were showing the Japs what they could do. For his part, General Tanaka fumed. By God, he'd teach 'em different, he swore to himself, once they came fully under his control. Why, they were a disgrace to the army, tumbling about like that, missing the step, not observing the cadence that was being shouted at the Indians by the few Japanese NCOs attached to the division.

Carried away by the sight, neither those on the podium nor those in the crowd noticed the coolie with the rusty bicycle who had now pushed his way through the Jews and had poised himself behind one of the tall Sikh policemen. Now, for some reason, the policeman's knees were buckling beneath him slowly and his turban was slipping down the side of his head in a slightly comic fashion. He looked as if he were fainting. In fact, as the coolie noted with satisfaction, the drug he had injected into the cop was acting faster than he had thought it would. Letting the drugged cop rest against his front wheel so that he remained upright still, the coolie hurriedly started to unscrew the crossbar. No one noticed. Who cared about ragged-arsed coolies in prosperous Singapore, anyway? They were the invisible people, weren't they . . . ?

Lyn breathed a sigh of relief. The limpet was attached at last. It had been a damned difficult task. The cruiser's lower hull was heavy with scum and barnacles; it had obviously not had a re-fit for years. It had taken the powerful magnets a hell of a time to penetrate through to the metal and hold the mine fast. Now they were functioning. But the delay had meant that the boats were in view of the surrounding ships in the full daylight once they had left the cover of the hull. Lyn knew that there was only one way he could ensure success now – and it was almost suicidal. He had to adjust the time fuse so that it went off within five minutes. That would mean the cruiser's crew would have no time to send down a diver to de-arm the mine once they had been spotted. At the same time, however, once the mine had exploded, every man and his bloody son would be shooting at them.

But even as he decided, he knew that he was risking the lives of his men as well as his own. He and Pongo were regulars. They were paid to chance getting killed in action. But not the Druid and Pongo's number two, whose name he couldn't recollect. So now he turned to the Druid and said, 'All right, you bloody Welshman, over the side.'

'Over the side, sir?'

'Yes, someone's got to survive once the Nips start throwing the shit at us. You're he.'

The Druid looked at him aghast. 'But why me, sir?' he stuttered, as Lyn prepared to move.

191

'Because you're the only one of us ignorant squaddies who can talk and write. You know what you bloody Taffies are like – you can talk a gee-gee's hind leg off. Someone's got to report what we've done – and it's you.'

'But—'

'No more buts – we've only got a matter of minutes left. Over the side with you and stick close to the hull. Work yourself to the land and then hope for the best. You've been a good bloke – for a Taffy.'

'But, sir . . .' the Druid's eyes suddenly brimmed with tears. He realized what the CO was saying. They were going to their deaths. He was being given a chance, perhaps a slim one, to survive.

Lyn wasted no more time. Catching the Druid completely off balance, he gave him a hefty push. Arms waving wildly, he went over the side with a splash. There was a cry of alarm from above. A moment later it was followed by a challenge. Lyn waited no longer. 'Come on, Pongo,' he called. 'Let's go . . . Good luck, Druid!' Next instant they were streaking out into the open bay. Almost immediately the Japs on deck started firing. Scarlet flashes stabbed the morning. Slugs hissed all about them, slicing up the water in vicious little bursts of white. Pongo was hit. 'Oh bugger it!' he cried, his arms flailing as he tried to stay upright. Lyn was struck in the shoulder. It was as if someone had hit him a bloody good whack with a cricket bat. He yelped with pain. He kept on going, trying to submerge the Sleeping Beauty. He couldn't. Temporarily he had lost the use of his left arm. He'd have to remain on the surface, a sitting duck for the Jap marines on the upper deck of the cruiser, pumping shot after shot after the two tiny craft. Lyn started to pray out loud. 'Please, God, destroy her . . . destroy her now—' The plea ended in another gasp. A bullet had struck him in the back. It slammed him to the gunwhale. For a moment he hung there helplessly and then he was up again, the brave little craft bearing him away steadily from that doomed ship. Behind him he left a dying Pongo and his already dead mate, sinking in the bullet-riddled Sleeping Beauty. Operation Malay Tiger was now almost concluded . . .

The coolie raised the improvised rocket launcher to his shoulder. His instructions from Australia had to be carried out still, though everything seemed to have gone wrong. Tanaka and his smart young assistant, Lieutenant Kimura, Australia HQ had believed, were the only ones who could jeopardize Operation Malay Tiger. Now his sister was in position, as he was. He hadn't the faintest idea if the saboteurs of Colonel Lyn's group were in position too. But orders were orders. The time had come for him to do his part.

Poor old Ma, his Japanese mother, hadn't a clue about what had been going on for a long time now, though she had always thought it strange that he hired himself out as a common coolie, he who was half Japanese and, if he had played his cards right, could have had a good job working for the Nips. He slid the home-made rocket into the muzzle of the tube, still covered by the dead Sikh policeman. He guessed it was the Aussie blood in him that had made him and his Sis take the risks they had done. Poor old Ma hadn't had a clue what the Kemptai had done to the old man when they had taken him back in 1942 when they had conquered Singapore. His dark face contorted with a mixture of misery and hatred as he remembered what the old man had looked like when they had finally released him from the prison. He had died two days later and it had been a mercy. No one should live with the indecent things they had done to Dad.

He peered through the home-made sight. He was pleased to see that Sis was standing well back from that bastard Tanaka, though she was a bit close to that so-clever Kimura-San, a very dangerous bugger, even if he was a Christian. Though how anyone could be a practising Christian and work for the torturers of the Kemptai, he had never been able to work out.

The coolie who wasn't a coolie drew a deep breath. He knew he might well be beaten to death by the Indians and the Japs in the next few minutes, but it didn't matter. He had to take his revenge – and he was sacrificing himself for the old country, Australia. He took first pressure on the trigger, peering down the sight. 'All right, you bastards,' he muttered to himself. 'Frigging well try this on for collar size!' He pressed the trigger.

The primitive rocket launcher exploded on his shoulder. Red flame stabbed the air. The missile, a hurrying black tube, sped towards the podium.

Later, when he had recovered, Lieutenant Kimura told the Allied correspondents and interrogators that he had actually seen the missile hurtling towards them. He maintained that the deadly rocket had been impressed on his mind's eye for all time. Then he had thought it was to be almost the last thing he ever would see. He knew immediately what it was. He drew his pistol in the same instant that all hell broke loose as the crowd panicked and the Indian volunteers started firing wildly, crying, '*We are betrayed . . . We are being attacked!*'

The tall Japanese-Australian went down the next instant, his face a bloody mess from the dum-dum bullet* which

---

*A bullet named after the Indian township of Dum Dum. A cross has been carved out of its nose so that it splatters cruelly on impact, causing a massive wound.

had exploded in it at close range, so that it looked as if someone had thrown a handful of strawberry jam at it.

But as he went down, sprawled arms extended over the rusty frame of his Raleigh like some latterday Jesus on a metal cross, he saw through the blood-red mist which was threatening to submerge him that the hated Tanaka was still on his feet. 'Sis,' he croaked, although he knew even in this dying moment that she could not possibly hear him. 'Croak the bastard . . . Don't let him get away . . . Croak—' The blood welled up in his throat in a bright-red torrent sparkling in the sun, and he drowned there in his own life juices . . .

The heavy cruiser shook violently like a kid's toy boat. Smoke started to seep through suddenly ruptured plates. The hull bulged. Once more the Japanese ship was racked by a great metallic shudder. A radio mast came tumbling down to the deck in a shower of blue electric sparks. Sailors started to yell. They ran back and forth in confusion, the deck heaving and tilting frighteningly under their running feet. Up at the machine-gun post behind the bridge, the gunner swept the sea with one last burst before he too fled in panic.

Colonel Lyn gasped with shock. The Sleeping Beauty started to sink immediately. He didn't care. He was dying. But he'd done it. By God, he'd done it! 'For King and country.' The solemn words of his old prep-school headmaster swept into his fading brain for some reason that he no longer had time to explain. 'For King and country,' he gasped. 'For King and country . . .'

Next moment the cruiser blew up with a great roar that seemed to go on and on for ever, and two miles away the end came just as swiftly and violently. Iris, bleeding

195

from a cut on her forehead, clasped the staggering General Tanaka to herself. It was no lovers' embrace; this was an embrace of death. Easily the razor-sharp blade of the deadly stiletto penetrated between his lower ribs, as they had shown her how. Tanaka's back arched like the string of a taut bow. He gasped almost as if he were experiencing unbelievable sexual delight. Gasping herself, she withdrew the knife with an awful sucking noise. The blade gleamed a bright red for an instant. Then she plunged it in one more time. Tanaka screamed shrilly in his final agony. His legs buckled beneath him. His body went limp against hers. She staggered back under his weight, blundered into a blinded, bleeding Kimura, who was sobbing and crying, 'Don't, Iris . . . please don't, Iris.' Too late! The young staff officer, his gold lanyard swinging wildly as he hauled back with his silver samurai sword, swept it forward. That keen blade bit and cut right into the back of her neck . . .

The cruiser had gone now in a tumult of wild water. The channel was empty now save for the mass of floating wreckage, the dead – and the lone man alternately singing in Welsh and sobbing and sobbing, as if his very heart would break . . .

Author's Note

Anybody who's read my other stuff knows I'm all heart. I bleed for my fellow human beings – all save politicians and publishers, of course; they're not human! But even 'Dour Dunc', as I'm known in the business, can squeeze out the odd tear now and again, however much it hurts. So I must admit when I saw the two old geezers get off the plane at Heathrow last month, the old glassy orbs were a trifle damp.

There they were, 'the Druid', as he was once known, now the Very Reverend Ap-Jones of the Church of Wales no less, bowed down with age and medals, just helping his one-time enemy, ex-Lieutenant Kimura, down the stairs. The poor old devil's been blind these sixty years or so now. The old lump came up in the old throat to see the Welshman directing Kimura and his white cane from step to step. I felt the urgent need to have a quick one. Sentimentality always does that to me. As I've said, I'm all heart.

Anyhow, I controlled myself and stayed for the chat. Old Druid was true to form. He said he was going to quote Churchill. I thought, Oh Christ, here he goes. He's going to do the Welsh bit about Churchill having troops shoot at their striking miners back in the '20s. But no, it wasn't that at all. He quoted Churchill saying, 'In the hour of struggle, policy is blinded by the passion of the struggle.

Yet the struggle with the enemy is over. There is then only the struggle with oneself. That is the hardest of all.'

That went down well with the bleeding heart from the *Guardian* at least. But I suppose it was apt. Kiss and make up sort of thing – and if those two veterans could do it, I suppose those of us who didn't fight in that war can. So it was good to see the two old enemies reconciled. But then Very Reverend started on religion, all that chapel sort of thing, in his Welsh sing-song, and I thought it was time to hie it to the Mucky Duck – the Black Swan to you – and swallow a couple of swift balls o' malt to the lads who were never reconciled. After all you can take this bleeding-heart stuff a bit too far sometimes, can't you . . . ?